Claude Lightfoot

OR HOW THE PROBLEM WAS SOLVED

"My God!" cried the atheist, jumping back and falling against Jordan. "What's that?"

Claude Lightfoot

OR HOW THE PROBLEM WAS SOLVED

By

Fr. Francis J. Finn, S.J.
AUTHOR OF TOM PLAYFAIR, PERCY WYNN, HARRY DEE, ETC.

TAN BOOKS AND PUBLISHERS, INC.
Rockford, Illinois 61105

Copyright © 1893 by Benziger Brothers, Inc., New York.

Retypeset and published in 2003 by TAN Books and Publishers, Inc.

ISBN 0-89555-712-6

Library of Congress Control No.: 2001-132398

Cover illustration © 2002 by Phyllis Pollema-Cahill. Cover illustration rendered expressly for this book and used by arrangement with Wilkinson Studios, Chicago.

Cover design by Peter Massari, Rockford, Illinois.

Printed and bound in the United States of America.

TAN BOOKS AND PUBLISHERS, INC.
P.O. Box 424
Rockford, Illinois 61105
2003

"It's so hard to imagine almost any small boy changing into a man, but in most you can see a faint streak of seriousness. But Claude strikes me as being the concentrated essence of small boy, and I can't even begin to imagine how or when he'll change."

—Page 16

CONTENTS

CHAPTER XVIII

CHAPTER XIX

CHAPTER XX

CHAPTER XXI

CHAPTER XXII

CHAPTER XXIII

CHAPTER XXIV

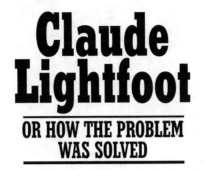

Claude Lightfoot

OR HOW THE PROBLEM WAS SOLVED

Chapter I

"THAT newcomer's a queer boy," observed John Winter.

"He's lively as a kitten," said Rob Collins. "I've been keeping an eye on him ever since the beginning of recess, and I don't think there's a square foot of ground in the college yard he hasn't passed over. He's tripped up five or six fellows already and just managed to get off being kicked at least twice. I think," added Rob solemnly, and bringing into use the latest knowledge he had gleaned from a passing fit of attention in Chemistry class, "I really do think that he's one of the Mercury Compounds."

Whereupon Frank Elmwood, the third of the group, rang a "chestnut bell," in answer to which Rob indignantly disclaimed any attempt at joking.

"Look," exclaimed John, breaking in upon the playful dispute of these two bosom friends, "your Compound of Mercury is going to get into trouble, I'm afraid; he's fooling around Worden!"

"Worden will kick him, sure," prophesied Rob.

"Yes, and hard, too, the overgrown bully," commented Frank, with a certain amount of bitterness in his voice and a frown upon his pale, energetic face.

The three speakers were leaning at ease against the storm door which opens upon the playground of Milwaukee College [that is, Academy]. It was ten o'clock recess, and the yard was everywhere alive with moving human figures. Like birds of swift passage, baseballs were flying through the air in all directions, and, on the run, of course, the multitudinous legs of small boys were moving from point to point. During recess the younger students seldom condescend to walk but, yielding to their natural and healthy inclinations, spend that quarter of an hour in a state of what is for the most part breathless animation. But among all these flying figures, the newcomer was eminently conspicuous. He seemed to move upon springs which, in their perfection, just fell short of wings.

On the way to Worden, he startled Charlie Pierson, the quietest lad in the college, by leaping clean over his shoulders. Charlie had been standing engrossed in watching a game, his head bent forward, his hands clasped behind his back and, fortunately for the nonce, his legs spread so as to afford him a good purchase for the shock, when, without warning, the young madcap came flying over his head.

"Confound your cheek!" cried Charlie, the lazy, benevolent smile on his face almost disappearing; "if I catch you, I'll pound your muscle till it's sore!" And as he spoke, he took after the dancing madcap.

"Whoop! Hi! Hi! Catch me," sang out Rob's Chemical Compound, as with his head craned so as to keep his pursuer in sight, he broke into a swift run, followed heavily and clumsily by Charlie, who was not given to hard exercise.

Now it so happened that Dan Dockery, a lively lad and intimate friend of Charlie, had been intently watching the proceedings of the young vaulter. Taking advantage of the fleeing boy's position of head, Dan planted himself, without being observed, in the path of the runner. As he had desired, a collision followed. Dan staggered back a few steps, while the lively youth bounded to one side like a rubber ball, rolled over and over, rose with a spring and a bound and, before Charlie could catch him, sprang away and dashed head first into the stomach of no less a person than the bully Worden.

For the moment, Worden lost all power of speech, but retained sufficient presence of mind to grasp his unwitting assailant in a vise-like grip.

Thus caught in the toils, the newcomer set about a process of wriggling and squirming which it is difficult to imagine and impossible to set down. Legs and arms writhed and bent, while the whole body twisted and turned in every conceivable posture, till the eye became dazed and blurred in following the swift changes. But Worden, still choking and gasping, held on grimly. The small boy who butted *him* in the stomach was not likely to forget the incident to the last day of his life.

"You wretched little rowdy!" he began, recovering his breath and endeavoring to put his captive into a position where he could best be kicked, "I'll teach you a lesson."

By way of reply, the small boy effected a miraculous wriggle which brought him through Worden's legs and rendered the intended operation of kicking, for the time being, impracticable. But Worden still preserved his hold and at once made a strenuous effort to bring the wriggler back into position.

At this point Pierson and Dockery, who despised Worden, as bullies are wont to be despised by the small boy, came to the rescue.

They sang in unison,

> Worden, Worden
> Went a-birdin'
> On a summer's day:
> Worden, Worden, went a-birdin'
> And the birds they flew away.

And then by way of chorus, a dozen youngsters in the vicinity chimed in with—

> Worden, Worden went a-birdin'
> And didn't *he* run away.

This was too much for the hero of these doggerels: releasing his intended victim, he started off in chase of his serenaders.

The cause of all this disturbance now made directly for the trio, who were still leaning against the storm door.

"What a stout pair of legs he's got!" exclaimed Collins. "And he moves with such ease. I never saw a little chap in knee breeches yet that looked so strong and so graceful."

"Yes," assented Elmwood. "And at the same time, he has such a sunny face: it's a healthy face too. It's not too chubby, and his complexion is really fine."

"And look at the smile he wears," continued John Winter. "It's what I would call sympathetic."

"Ahem!" grunted Rob.

"I mean," said John coloring, "that it makes you feel jolly and gay to look at it. You can see from the straight way he holds himself and from his build that he's a mighty strong little chap. He looks *sunny*—that's the word. His hair is really sunny. He's really a pretty boy."

"Pshaw!" growled Frank, "sunniness may be the right word, but prettiness certainly isn't. Almost any little boy, who's dressed well and who's not thoroughly bad, looks pretty. But this little chap is interesting."

"Hallo, Specksy!" cried the object of these remarks, who had been staring at his critics for full half a minute.

Rob and John joined in a laugh at Frank's expense. Though only seventeen, Frank wore spectacles.

"Hallo, Sublimate of Mercury!"

"You're another, and twice anything you call me!" came the quick answer. "I say, I like this school immensely. There's a yard to it where a fellow's got room enough to move around in."

"What school did you go to before you

came here?" Frank inquired.

"Sixteenth District till a few days ago."

"What happened then?"

"I got expelled." As he made his answer, he favored Frank with a series of winks. He had blue eyes, not over-large, but with a snap and sparkle about them which added much to the sunshininess of his appearance.

"Stop your winking and tell us why you were expelled," pursued Frank.

The artless youth had been hopping about impatiently during this dialogue, and, as Frank put him the last question, he flew at John Winter, seized John's hat and, without further ado, took to his heels.

With an ejaculation expressive partly of amusement, partly of annoyance, John took after him. He was the youngest and smallest of the trio—indeed, though a member of the class of Poetry, he still went about in knickerbockers—but in running he was second to none of his class fellows. After a sharp pursuit, he captured the snatcher of hats and brought him back wriggling to Frank and Rob.

"Now," puffed John, retaining his firm grasp on our young friend's wrist, "tell us about your being expelled."

"I was expelled for nothing—there!" with

a wriggle. "Let me go, will you?" More wriggles. "Let me go, I say!" Still more wriggles. "Ow-w-w-w! Stop squeezing!"

And in a seeming paroxysm of pain, the wriggler fell into a complete state of collapse and hung limp, a dead weight from John's hand, while lines and spasms of pain chased about his most expressive face.

Softened by pity, John let go. In a flash, the limpness was gone, and the brightest, happiest, sunniest boy, his hair shot with gold and dancing to its owner's motions, was hopping and skipping before the three poets, his right thumb raised to his pretty little nose and four fingers wriggling like the fingers of an excited Italian in the heart of the Italian game of Mora.

"Yah! yah!—fooled you, didn't I? Oh, didn't I take him in, Specksy?"

"Tell us how you got expelled," said Rob, "and I'll give you some chocolate caramels."

There was a cessation of hop and skip.

"How many?"

"Five or six."

"Will you give me one to start on?"

Rob handed him a caramel.

"Now," continued the sunny one, as he put the candy in his mouth, "how'll I know that you'll give me the rest?"

"Well I suppose you can trust me."

"No, you don't. I know your brother Walter, and he says you're no good. You just pass those caramels over to Specksy; I like Specksy." And the frank young gentleman glanced at Elmwood with open admiration.

"All right, Johnny," said Rob, as he executed the condition.

"You needn't call me Johnny," continued the newcomer, sidling toward Frank and making a sudden but unsuccessful grab at the candy in his hand. "My name is Claude— Claude Lightfoot, and don't you forget it, Specksy."

In answer to this appeal, Frank gave him a caramel.

"We're not particular about your name," put in John Winter, anxious to quote

> What's in a name? That which we call
> a rose . . .

"Just what I was going to say," interrupted Elmwood, with a mischievous twinkle in his eye. "Go on, Claude, and tell us about your expulsion."

"It was all on account of a billy goat and a lightning rod."

"Ah!" said Rob. "Did the billy goat strike the lightning rod?"

Before replying, Claude extorted a third caramel from Frank.

"No, it didn't. Last Wednesday a fellow stumped me to bring my billy goat to school. General Jackson (that was his name) behaved like a gentleman as long as we were outside the school building. I tied him up in the yard; but just as soon as I started to go into school, General Jackson began to get frisky; and then the fellow that stumped me loosed him, and he came bumping in after me—"

"Who? The fellow that stumped you?"

"No, the General. I wanted to run him out; but a lot of fellows stood at the door and shooed at him. Then General Jackson got mad and went just a-tearing down that hall and sent a lot of girls a-squealing, and one or two of them sprawling; and I came charging after. Some of those girls said that I was setting him on. I caught the General after he had scared the wits out of two of the women teachers—one of 'em had her hand on her breast and it was heaving like anything, and the other was standing on a chair with her skirts gathered about her, the way they all do when they see a mouse. The principal came down on me then—"

"Where did he come down on you?"

"On my hands—both of them, and said

that next time I cut up, he'd expel me for being something or other—uncursable, I think he said."

"Incorrigible, you mean, Claude," suggested Winter.

"That's it. I only heard the word once, and I was too excited to notice how he said it. So I went home and made up my mind not to take any more risks. But the next day, a fellow stumped me just before class to climb up the lightning rod to the third story and offered me a big apple if I'd do it. I forgot to think, and caught hold of that lightning rod and began to climb it hand over hand—."

"Where did you learn to climb?" Frank inquired.

"I didn't learn at all, Specksy: it just came natural, I reckon. So I got up almost as high as the second story when one of those lady teachers saw me from a third story window. And maybe she didn't yell! Then a couple of other teachers, of course they were ladies, who heard her singing out, put their heads out, and they just howled, and I tell you I began to work my way down as fast as I knew how; but it was no use. Before I got to the ground, the principal was standing at the door and making eyes at me through his specks. When I got on my feet, he asked me whether I could find my way home. He was awful funny with me—"

"Sarcastic, you mean," said Rob.

"Maybe I do—anyhow it was a funny way of being funny. He told me never to show my face in that school again; and that fellow wouldn't give me the apple, either. He wouldn't even give me half. So I went home feeling bad about it all—"

"Especially about the apple," suggested Frank.

"That's so, Specksy; it was mean. I told Ma and Kate all about it. You see I wanted them to fix it all right with Pa, who's awful fond of the public schools."

"Did he go to the public schools himself?"

"No; he was born in Canada and didn't come here till he was twenty."

"Well, Claude," said Frank, "it's about time for you to come to a Catholic school anyhow."

"Sure. It suits me all over," answered Claude, who was now making repeated endeavors to touch the back of his neck with the sole of his right foot. "Ma's been wanting me to go ever since I left Miss Wilton's private school two months ago. She and my sister Kate are anxious for me to get ready for my First Communion. Pa was vexed and wanted to put me to work. When Ma and Kate won him over, then the President of this College didn't seem to care about taking a boy that had been expelled. Then I got a letter from Miss Wilton, and Kate had a long talk with the President, and now I'm here on trial. Pa says he hopes they'll expel me from this College too. But Pa is so careful about me; you see he wants me to be an American."

"Why," put in John, "were you born in New Zealand?"

"Aw, now, aren't you funny? I was born here just as much as you were, and twice as much too. Pa thinks that if a boy wants to be an American he's got to go to an American school."

"What's the matter with this college?" queried Rob.

"I don't know what's—" Here Claude sprang upon Elmwood's back and was within a little of bringing that dignified young gentleman to the ground. As Claude's evident intention was merely to demonstrate the warmth of his friendship, Frank contented himself with reaching back after Claude and setting the young bundle of nerves upon his feet again.

"If you don't behave yourself, sir," he said

with a suppressed smile, "I'll put you over my knee."

Claude was about to make some derisive comment upon this remark when suddenly his face changed, and he darted away like a minnow when it catches sight of a pike. Worden, in this instance, was the pike. He came rushing past the three poets with an expression of anticipatory triumph when Frank Elmwood caught him by the arm. Quick as thought young Winter, who was something of a wag and a tease, seized Worden's right hand and shook it warmly.

"How are you, Worden? Glad to see you!" cried John, with a malicious grin.

"And I say, Worden, old boy, you're losing your dignity," added Frank. "What's your hurry, anyhow?"

Worden, fully Frank's equal in size and weight, was meantime endeavoring to break away from the strong, nervous grasp upon his arm, and of two minds as to swearing at these grinning captors.

"Look here, Elmwood, let go. Drop my hand, Winter. Let go, I say. Let go. Conf— —you fellows are making a fool of me."

"They might just as well try to make a square circle," put in Rob, as with a bow and a smile he advanced to welcome amiable Mr. Worden, who for a wonder kept his temper, lest something worse should happen to him.

"Is the Mercury arrangement out of reach yet?" asked Frank of Rob.

"Sure! He's at the far end of the yard, trying to see how high he can kick."

"All right: you can go, Worden, and next time you get after a small boy, you heroic fraud, we hope you'll have worse luck than you had now."

Worden looked bowie knives at Frank, puffed his lower lip into a baby pout, stuck his thumbs in his vest and walked away with a sorry attempt at dignity. He made no further offer that day to wreak vengeance on Claude; for, although he was not a boy of fine discernment, there was something in the tone of Frank's voice which he recognized as a note of warning.

As Worden walked away, Frank's face settled into an expression of study. He took off his glasses and, while eyeing them with his severest look, rubbed them vigorously.

"A penny for your thoughts, Frank," ventured Rob.

"I'm thinking of that sunny scalawag who is now kicking his legs about as though there never had been a yesterday, and it never occurred to him that there'd be a tomorrow. He's bound to have hard times, just as sure as he lives to grow up. At present he has about as much sense of responsibility as a kitten. Now, I'm wondering how he'll develop. It's so hard to imagine almost any small boy changing into a man, but in most you can see a faint streak of seriousness. But Claude strikes me as being the concentrated essence of small boy, and I can't even begin to imagine how or when he'll change."

"Oh, I guess it'll come about in the ordinary way," said John Winter. "We were all small boys once—you needn't grin at me because I'm in knickerbockers. I can write verses and essays—and yet three years ago, I used to wonder how boys in Poetry class could do those things."

"I think you've given the true solution," said Rob. "We change with years: and Claude will take his medicine just as we did and change in the usual way."

"I don't believe it: I can't imagine it," said Frank.

And Frank was right. Claude's change was not to be the work of time. The difficulties of that change, its seeming impossibility and its sudden accomplishment form the subject matter of this narrative.

Chapter II

*IN WHICH CLAUDE ATTRACTS THE ATTENTION
OF HIS TEACHER*

CLAUDE, during the morning hour preceding recess, had passed through all the formalities required of a newcomer. It was after his first interview with our three poets that he made his first appearance in the class of Third Academic.

Frank Elmwood had discovered a problem in Claude; it devolved upon the teacher of Third Academic to attempt the solution. Mr. Grace was an excellent teacher. In point of order, his was a model class; and his pupils, with scarcely an exception, were impressed by the piety and devotion which he taught by example as well as by word. But his influence was by no means in keeping with the respect which he inspired. Many of his scholars—all his lively boys, in fact—were content with simply admiring him. They did not understand their teacher; he did not understand them. His words of counsel, his exhortations failed to reach their hearts. They revered Mr. Grace; they esteemed him; they would be willing, were the matter directed to their attention, to sign a petition for his

speedy canonization and to give witness to
his heroic virtues: but the heights of their
admiration reached that thinner air where
there is no thriving growth of imitation.

Mr. Grace had never been a real boy. He
had grown from childhood to manhood with
his eyes fixed upon the upper realms. His
school companions had called him a saint,
and, unstinted in their words of praise, had
subjected him to all manner of teasing. Without meaning it, they had frequently not
stopped short of downright cruelty. The
"saint" had borne his trials with such open-
eyed wonder and unchanging meekness that
he had in the long run subdued nearly all
his tormentors. Nevertheless, these petty per-
secutions had left upon him an indelible
impression. He had noticed, without accounting for the fact, that there were two kinds
of boys—boys that teased him, and boys that
did not. His observations moving a step further had led him to perceive that those who
teased him were wild, noisy, full of life, and
that those who did not were gentle, quiet
and pleasant of manner. Now Mr. Grace had
nothing of the dramatic faculty. He could not
put himself in another's place. As a boy, he
could not understand his lively companions;
as a man he met with the same difficulty.

He still recognized but two classes, the wild and the quiet. He was too charitable to allow himself to think any boy with whom he had to deal really bad. But if he had been forced to a decision, he would certainly have classed all quiet boys as being good and all noisy boys as being bad: and after his first hour's experience with Claude, I dare say that he would have put that young gentleman's name at the very head of the latter list.

But if Mr. Grace failed to sympathize with the harum-scarums, he nonetheless managed them well. He was quite a disciplinarian, and his firmness and method succeeded— only partially, it is true—in atoning for his invincible lack of insight.

Mr. Grace took in at a glance something of the excessive liveliness which distinguished Claude at this period of his development and, in consequence, seated the young wriggler on the front bench which directly faced the professorial chair. Before the end of an hour, Mr. Grace discovered that, in the way of fidgeting, he had sadly underestimated Claude's capacities.

And yet Claude was clearly on his best behavior; he opened his book with a fixed expression of resolve upon his face, and following each word with his finger end and with a painstaking movement and mumbling of the lips, he thus entered upon his college career with an output of zeal too intense to stand the wear and tear of many minutes. It was the hour assigned for Arithmetic class, and Mr. Grace had allowed his scholars five minutes to memorize the rule for compound proportion.

Before half of that time had expired, Claude raised his head and, fixing his dancing eyes full upon his teacher, snapped his fingers: forty boys grinned quietly and became interested.

"Sh!" warned the teacher.

"I know that rule, Mister. Just hear me say it."

An unmistakable giggle went from one end of the room to the other: it was short-lived, for Mr. Grace's stern glance was the signal for perfect stillness.

Mr. Grace left his seat and, bending over Claude, whispered in his ear:

"My boy, no one is allowed to snap his fingers in this class—there's no need of making such a noise. If you want to call my attention to anything, simply hold up your hand. Again, no one should speak in class, not even to me, without permission."

Claude was crushed. It was not the substance of what was said that subdued him, but the manner. The quiet, subdued whisper is the strongest weapon against a young-ster's boisterousness. If he shout and the professor answer in kind, the confusion gath-ers force: but a whisper in return, a quiet look—these are too much. Mr. Grace knew this secret of discipline, and, I must confess, sometimes employed it to the verge of cru-elty. His method of maintaining order gave no outlet to the overflow of animal spirits: he had never suffered from such an over-flow himself.

Claude, with an injured expression, again bent his eyes on his book, while one hand went up absently to the top of his head and the other to his chest. The former hand began patting the fair hair, while the latter moved up and down. It was quite a feat to do this— any boy reader knows how hard it is—and Charlie Pierson and Dan Dockery, seated behind our hero, were in a subdued ecstasy of delight at Claude's deftness. Still conning his book, Claude's hands absently reversed their motions, the upper hand doing the rub-bing, the other the patting. Charlie felt tempted to applaud and Dan gave a snicker.

"Take your hand off your head and stop fidgeting," whispered Mr. Grace.

"I ain't doing nothing."

"Study, then."

"I know this—"

"Sh!"

Then this poor victim of classroom discipline innocently twirled his thumbs—one going in the opposite direction to the other. Mr. Grace allowed this proceeding simple tolerance. The five minutes being up, the teacher required all to close their books and, beginning with the boy in the furthest bench, heard the recitation. While the first boy called upon was hesitating on the last three words of the rule, Claude received the following note:

> Anybody can twirl his thumbs. Why don't you wag one of your ears?
> DAN DOCKERY

Before he had torn this note to pieces, one of Claude's ears twitched, quivered and actually did wag. Restraint was no longer possible: Dockery, Pierson and some half dozen boys broke into a roar. Mr. Grace had not witnessed the moving of the ear, but he perceived from the fact that the laughers were watching Claude that the cause of the disturbance was on the front bench.

"Come here, Claude."

With a skip and a bound, which nearly upset the class dignity for the second time, Claude was at the teacher's desk.

"Why are you trying to disturb the class?"

"I'm not trying to disturb anything. I was just trying to make my ears work, and one of them wouldn't go."

There are professors who would have had some difficulty in keeping serious after this naive confession. Not so Mr. Grace. He looked upon the lively boy as being capable of saying or doing anything. He never knew what the small boy might say or do at any given moment, but it was all one to him: he was ever expecting the unexpected. So he received this explanation with unimpaired seriousness.

"It's a great loss of time for you, Claude, to give so much attention to your ears. This is the place for learning, not for gymnastics. Go to your seat, and keep quiet."

"I can't, Mister."

"Try your best, Claude: if at first you don't succeed, I'll help you with a few lines to memorize." And Mr. Grace smiled very sweetly.

Claude, on resuming his seat, caught hold of his desk with both hands, determined to reduce those unruly members to subjection, and set about paying attention in a fresh spurt of zeal. He seemed to forget that he

had legs and feet, however, and kicked energetically into the air, one little foot and then
another flying up flush with the top of his
desk.

Mr. Grace, while hurrying through the
recitations, ignored these demonstrations.

"Now," said the teacher, when all had been
heard, "if Claude will be good enough to put
his feet where they belong and pay attention, I'll show you how to carry out the rule
you have just memorized."

Claude was taken aback to such an extent
that he could make no reply. He had been
all attention. He had had his eyes fixed on
Mr. Grace and had devoured his every feature. And in truth, Claude had been
impressed with the fine, low, broad brow,
under the mass of soft chestnut hair; with
the noble eye, clear, steady, unmistakably
frank; with the handsome oval of the face,
pale and somewhat thin, yet revealing in its
every line the student and the ascetic. Not
a trait escaped his keen, quick, inquisitive
eyes. What struck him most of all was the
air of holiness upon Mr. Grace's features,
and just as he was making up his mind that
he liked a man teacher far better than he
liked any woman teacher, there came this
stinging rebuke.

How in the world could he be expected to keep track of his legs while bending all his forces to bring into proper subjection his hands and fingers and head and ears, and at the same time follow everything that was going on in class?

But he was not utterly discouraged. Fastening a steady gaze upon his mischievous legs, and bringing his hands folded before him so that he could embrace them in the same glance, he resolved not to move a muscle till the end of class. It was an heroic determination. And indeed after three minutes—the while Mr. Grace went on working out in all calmness a problem at the blackboard—there was hardly a part of Claude's anatomy which did not claim his attention. There was an ache here, and a cramp there; his face itched, his feet threatened to go asleep, and Claude was morally certain, early as was the season, that a fly was disporting upon his neck. Ah, if he could only capture that fly! One minute passed in this state of torture; the perspiration began to gather on the young hero's cheek. A new ache, another itch, another fly—so it appeared to Claude—then a host of itches seemed to swoop down upon him, till at length the poor boy could no longer stand under a fire so galling. He gave one wriggle and, half-rising from his seat, stretched himself at full length, ending the performance with a great sigh of relief, while class and professor watched him with rounded eyes.

"Yawning isn't allowed," whispered Mr. Grace at his ear.

"Can I go out, sir?"

"No; you've only been in ten minutes."

"Let me go to the board and do a sum, then. I know how it's done."

Mr. Grace did not quite understand this young gentleman's trouble; but by good fortune, someone had to go to the board, and in consideration of the fact that Claude was a newcomer, he granted him this last request. Our little wriggler was now in his element. Snatching up a blackboard eraser, he hopped from one end of the board to the other—it extended the full length of the room—rubbing out everything in his track with a superfluous energy and ceasing regretfully from his labor when there was nothing more to erase.

No sooner had Mr. Grace enunciated the problem than, in a fever of energy, Claude jotted down the conditions and, not without many hops, extraordinary bendings of the legs and much flying of chalk dust, which powdered his face, worked it out perfectly.

"Please, Mister, give me another one!"

"Couldn't you first explain the various steps you have taken?"

"Oh, yes, sir!" Whereupon our little Claude, who was very nimble of tongue and by no means timid, launched into an explanation, which he accompanied with some very expressive wriggles. His request too was granted. Mr. Grace, who was studying how to reduce this piece of animation to discipline, thought that a half hour at the blackboard might throw some light on the question. So Claude got himself into layers of chalk, and hopped about ecstatically, and succeeded in showing that he was really first rate in arithmetic. When he returned to his seat, he was quite quiet, and beyond daubing his nose unintentionally with a bit of ink and dropping all his books with a thud upon the floor, the last quarter of his first hour in class was in every way commendable.

Chapter III

*IN WHICH CLAUDE SURPRISES
HIS SISTER KATE, AND JOHN WINTER
SURPRISES EVERYBODY*

AT twenty-nine minutes past three, a small boy was bending the crab and diversifying this exercise by walking on his hands in front of the Notre Dame convent school. At half after three, a bell sounded and the small acrobat, jumping to his feet, picked up his books and stationed himself at the school door.

Presently the girls came trooping out, talking volubly according to the amiable manners of their sex and time of life. The small boy did not seem to concern himself with the musical stream of chatter, nor did he bestow more than a cursory glance upon any one of the talkers, till his eye lighted upon a little Miss of fifteen smiling and silent among the chatterers.

"Hi Kate!" he shouted, and with unintentional rudeness he elbowed a young lady aside and gave Kate a brotherly kiss.

"Why, Claude," exclaimed Kate in astonishment, "what brought you here?"

"My feet, Kate: both of them. You see, I

wanted to surprise you. I've come to take you home, and I'm going to come every afternoon. See! I've kept it secret all day. Mama was in it, and she likes it ever so much. The College lets out at three, and it gives me just time enough to come here and catch you. We'll have great times going home together every afternoon."

Kate's eyes shone with delight, and her pretty cheeks took on a deeper flush and dimpled into smiles. No one looking at the two would fail, even in a passing glance, to perceive their relationship; and no one watching them in this short change of greetings would hesitate to say that if ever brother and sister loved each other and were proud of each other, that brother and sister were Claude and Kate.

There was the same complexion, Kate's being a trifle more delicate; the same facial expression. The girl, older by three years, was far maturer. Her eyes were very bright, very blue, and as they gazed into Claude's face, very tender. She lacked, of course, much of Claude's liveliness—and it was well she did. One can stand only a certain amount even from a boy, and Claude exceeded that. The easy good nature of Claude appeared in her softened and refined. People would style it sweetness, and, were it not that the word has been cheapened, I could sum up the description of Claude's sister by saying that she was a sweet girl.

Claude had a good mother. She had fostered by every art and device the love between this happy-go-lucky lad and the wiser sister. She had happily succeeded, and these two little ones knew each other's hearts and loved each other in fullness of measure.

The vision and memory of Kate was the most effectual breakwater to Claude's extravagance. He knew that he was to render her an account, and often he paused on the verge of some daring scheme, checked by the image of her sweet, sad, reproving face.

"It was so kind of you, Claude," said Kate. "It will make the last hour of class pass lightly to think that you are on the way to meet me as I come out. And then such talks as we'll have on the way home."

"Yes; it'll be immense! And look here, Kate, it'll make *me* behave the last hour of class; or I'll be put in 'jug' and won't have a chance to come and take you home."

At this point Claude, reversing the conventional etiquette, put his arm through his sister's, and Kate was too overjoyed to correct this breach of decorum, as they walked gayly down the street toward the river which divided the East side of the city from the West.

"What's the 'jug,' Claude?"

"That's what the fellows call it. If you're kept in by your teacher, you've got to stay in after class in one of the classrooms and work out your punishment. All the other fellows who are kept in have to go to the same room. That's the jug, and it keeps going for half an hour."

"You must try to keep out of that, Claude, or it will spoil everything."

"I came near being in jug this afternoon, all the same," remarked Claude, going a little out of his way and dragging Kate after him in order to give a stray oyster can an energetic kick.

"Did you?"

"Yes. My teacher Mr. Grace is a nice man, and he looks like a saint. All the chaps in our class say so, even those who are down on him. But he is awful correct. He wants a fellow to be just so. He doesn't give me any chance. If he'd only get mad, I wouldn't mind. But he looks so nice and quiet. Once when he came up to me, he was smiling—and that's the time he came down on me hardest. The boys in our class say he never gets rattled; but look out for him when he smiles and looks very amiable. Dan Dockery said a funny thing, Kate; he said, 'When an Indian goes on the warpath, he puts on his war paint, but Mr. Grace puts on a smile.' Well, after class Mr. Grace called me, and he looked so nice and amiable, I thought he was going to give me something. He said, 'Claude, you've been very troublesome today, and you'd better go to jug now and write one hundred times "I MUST NOT FIDGET IN CLASS."' Now that was awful hard, Kate, for I had been looking forward all day to springing this surprise on you. So I tried to beg off. I said I had done my best, and he smiled. I said it was my first day, and he smiled. I said I wouldn't do it any more, and he looked just like a picture saint. Then I felt like crying: and I out and told him the whole truth."

"That's where you should have begun, dear," said Kate.

"I guess it was, Kate. As soon as I told him how anxious I was to meet my sister, he stopped smiling and began to think. Then he said I might go."

While Kate and Claude are crossing the Grand Avenue bridge, it may be worthwhile accounting for Mr. Grace's act of mercy.

"This boy," he had reflected, "needs all the

influence of his sister to tone him down. If he walks home with her every afternoon, he will not be tempted to break lamp posts, ring doorbells and steal rides on streetcars."

As they walked along the Avenue on the "West Side," Claude narrated every circumstance of his day's adventures, from the first hour of class to the last, when he disturbed the ranks by jumping over a boy's head.

Kate listened with interest and sympathy. She had no word of blame for her little darling, but she stood up for Mr. Grace.

"You must try to like your teacher very much, Claude," she said in her quiet, earnest way. "It's the first time you've ever had a religious* for a teacher, and you need a little piety, dear."

"That's so," answered Claude, resisting a temptation to vault over a hitching post. "And you should have heard him in Catechism class. You could see that he was in dead earnest, and he spoke so nicely."

Claude's appreciation was just. Mr. Grace was at his best in teaching Christian Doctrine. Were it not for his want of sympathy for the wilder lads, which many of them

---

* Apparently Mr. Grace is a Jesuit scholastic, that is, a man who has taken vows in the Society of Jesus but has not yet been ordained a priest. —*Publisher*, 2003.

returned with reverential dislike, Mr. Grace through his devout instructions might have bound each and every one by the golden chain of love to the feet of God.

"And remember, Claude," continued Kate, "that to those who don't understand you, you are a very troublesome boy. Mr. Higgins, our next-door neighbor, thinks you ought to be in jail; don't you remember how he told you the other day that he thought you were possessed by the devil?"

Claude's voice rippled into a silvery wave of laughter, and in the brief spell of mirth he so far forgot himself as to take a flying leap over a large box of goods which they happened to be passing.

"Is that the way you intend to escort me home, dear?" asked Kate with her gentle smile.

"Oh, I beg pardon, Kitty; I clean forgot. When you reminded me of Mr. Higgins, I could have jumped over a telegraph pole almost."

"Claude," continued Kate, "you haven't told me about the most important thing of all."

"I know it," said Claude, on the point of clapping his sister on the back, "and I kept it back a-purpose."

"Tell me, dear: I've been thinking about it all day."

"The vice president says that I'm just in time: they began the First Communion class about two weeks ago. The First Communion day is to be on the last Sunday in May, and today is the thirtieth of April. There are ten boys besides myself in First Communion class."

"So, dear, we've only a month to get ready: we must pray hard and be very good."

"Yes, Kate, we'll do our best: I'm a little afraid, though. They put off a boy if he doesn't behave well: and, Kitty, it's so hard for me to behave when you're not around."

Kate felt prompted to kiss the little man out of hand, but Grand Avenue was a crowded thoroughfare. In lieu of this she patted the muscular arm which was drawn through hers.

"And there's another thing, Kitty; we'll have to begin to study our Latin after supper."

"I've begun already," said Kate.

"What!" cried Claude, leaping into the air (considerately taking his arm out of Kate's in doing so) and bringing his heels together three distinct times.

"Now, Claude! Well, I began one week ago at the Latin. As soon as Papa made up his mind to send you to college, I knew we'd have to begin Latin, so I made a start at once, in order to help my frisky little brother.

There now. That's *my* surprise."

"Kitty, you're a darling."

And it was with some difficulty that Kate succeeded in keeping her brother from openly testifying his gratification in a demonstrative hug.

They were now passing the Public Library, and Claude's quick eye caught sight of two young men as they stepped off the elevator at the entrance of that building.

"Why, Kitty, here are two of the boys I was telling you about. Hi! Frank—John!"

The two poets, each with a book under his arm, turned to see the Mercury Compound, all motion as to his lively legs, pirouetting beside a girl.

"I'm glad we've met you. I've just been telling my sister about you two and Rob Collins, and she wants to know you. Kate, this is Frank Elmwood, and this is John Winter. They're poets, and I guess they write poetry books."

Kate held out her hand gracefully to each and clearly showed that she was pleased to meet her brother's friends.

"I'm glad to meet you, Mr. Elmwood, and—" Kate paused, for Winter was in knee breeches—"and Mr. Winter."

"If you are, call us Frank and John,"

laughed Frank, his eyes twinkling behind his spectacles.

John Winter was not quite at his ease. He was a bashful youngster and, not knowing what to do with his arms, put them akimbo, and blushed still more.

"Claude was telling me about his brush with Worden and how you two came to his help. It was very nice of you."

"We—eh—we fooled Worden bad," blurted out John, still with his arms akimbo and wondering what was the matter with his feet. On uttering this profound remark, John blushed more violently than before and asked himself mentally what the young lady with the clear blue eyes thought of his grammar.

"It was very nice of you and Frank, John," said Kate, making an endeavor, not altogether unsuccessful, to put the unhappy youngster at his ease. "My brother Claude is very thoughtless and is constantly getting into quarrels."

"That's so, Kit," assented Claude with penitence in his voice.

"He and I have agreed never to begin a quarrel," continued the girl—whereupon a broad grin came over Frank's face. The idea of Kate's identifying herself with Claude in his quarrels was too much for his sense of humor. Kate laughed in return.

"It sounds funny to you," continued Kate, "but I've got into the habit of talking about Claude's affairs as though they were mine. So Claude and I never start a quarrel, but sometimes we forget ourselves and put other boys out of patience, and then we find ourselves striking back, don't we, Claude?"

"Yes, we do," answered Claude quite seriously.

Frank laughed, and John, who had now put his hands out of sight in his pockets, broke into a smile.

"And then Claude comes home with a swollen nose, or puffed-out lip—and generally with his clothes torn, even if he escapes fighting."

"I'm pretty hard on clothes," said Claude. "I'll bet the Sign of the Blue Flag makes money on me."

"If you're walking up town," said Kate to her new acquaintances, "we might all go together, and Claude will tell you how he was measured for the pair of knee-breeches he's wearing now."

"I live on the East Side," Frank made answer, "but I'm on my way to John's to borrow his Latin themes. In our class John is the great authority in theme work."

Frank, as he spoke, glanced maliciously at John, who, of course, blushed again.

"He's stuffing—oh, goodness—he's exaggerating, Claude," answered John, directing the first part of the sentence to the sister, and turning the conclusion full upon Claude.

Kate could scarcely refrain from laughing.

"Now," said Frank, as they took their way up the Avenue, "tell us about how you bought those pants, Claude."

"You begin, Kit, and we'll do it together."

"Very well: when we settled that Claude was to go to college, mama wanted to start him in with a new outfit. So yesterday Claude went down to the Blue Flag, with permission to do his own buying. When Claude entered the store, a clerk came up to him— they all know him there—and asked him what he wanted. 'I want to see the boss,' said Claude. 'He's busy,' said the clerk. 'All right, I'll wait.' The clerk went away then, and after a while the senior partner came out. He's very fond of us, and when he saw Claude he laughed."

"Yes," put in Claude, "and he said, 'You were here only two weeks ago. If all little boys wore out clothes like you, I'd have been a millionaire long ago.' And then he asked me what I wanted. I told him that I wanted a pair of pants that would fit me so's I could put my foot around my neck. You see the last pair I bought fitted for everything except that, and I can't enjoy myself if I can't put my foot about my neck."

"And then," continued Kate, "the proprietor called out to know whether there were any knee breeches in the establishment with copper plating and brass finishings."

Kate paused to laugh, and you may be sure her merriment found a fine echo in Claude.

"Of course he was joking," explained Claude, "and the clerk, he laughed till he shook all over. Then the boss hustled around himself, and got me these. I put them on in the little green dressing room and came out feeling jolly."

"And then, do you know what happened? The proprietor made Claude put both his feet around his neck."

"Whose neck, and whose feet?" asked Frank mischievously.

"Claude's neck and Claude's feet!" laughed Kate.

"Did he put both feet around at the same time?"

"No: one at a time, Frank."

"I'll bet I can put both around, all the

same," stated the object of this narrative in his matter-of-fact way.

"And then when Claude said that the clothes were good for that sort of exercise, the man made him put his foot in his mouth, turn a handspring and bend the crab. Claude was delighted. The proprietor, who is a friend of Papa's, told us all about it last night. He said, 'I've made a hit with one customer anyhow. Claude has made me promise to wait on him personally whenever he comes, because I know the right way to find out whether a small boy's knee breeches fit him.'"

"That's so," added Claude. "Lots of clerks seem to think that all a boy wants pants for is to stand around in."

"Well, Kate," said Frank, "John and I turn here. We're very glad to have met you, and you may rely upon it that if we can help Claude, we will do so."

"Thank you very much. I'm so glad that Claude has found such kind friends among Catholic boys," said Kate warmly. "So far he has had few *boy* friends. Won't you come up some evening and take tea with us? Mama will be delighted and Claude really needs some friends."

Kate made this request very earnestly. During the foregoing conversation she had been studying the faces of the two poets. John, she perceived, with his smooth ruddy face, was bashful, timid, rather immature, and yet not without a fair sense of humor. Frank was ready, quick, honest and energetic. Energetic: that was his predominant trait. His lips were thin, his mouth firm, and his pale features, relieved from a touch of austerity by the twinkling eye, gave him the air of a thorough student, as indeed he was.

"Certainly, we shall be glad to call," answered Frank.

"Well, good afternoon."

"Good evening, sir," added John, addressing himself to Kate.

John almost broke into a run after this effort.

"You remember the problem concerning Claude that I broached this morning?" asked Frank, putting his hand on the shoulder of his now fiery-faced companion.

"I remember," said John, "that I put my foot into it every time I got a chance."

"Oh, bother! Kate saw you were bashful and appreciated your condition. She's a good girl, and if that brother of hers is to be saved at all, she's the one to do the saving. Yes, John, Kate solves the problem."

"I guess so," answered John moodily.

As the sequel will show, Kate did not solve the problem.

———————

Chapter IV

*IN WHICH CLAUDE CULTIVATES THE
ACQUAINTANCE OF MR. RUSSEL AND BECOMES
A MEMBER OF THE "HIGHFLIERS"*

ALTHOUGH Claude was an object of secret terror to Mr. Grace, he by no means produced the same dread feeling in the bosom of Mr. Russel, the first prefect of the yard. Mr. Russel was a genial man; his face in ordinary moments was a smiling one, or, at least, gave promise of a smile; and it was his great delight to chaff the little boys. He wore such an air of good nature that youngsters not well acquainted with him sometimes ventured upon taking liberties. The experiment was seldom repeated by the same boy, for the face, so smiling before, looked down upon the youthful offender with a dignity and an air of command which made words on Mr. Russel's part unnecessary.

Claude was a welcome addition to the prefect's list of little friends. He watched with interest this attempt at perpetual motion as he flew around the playground, and was not a little amused at the freshness and variety of Claude's antics.

"There's a boy for you," he remarked to Elmwood.

"I think it's several boys rolled into one," answered Frank. "He's made away with six different hats in the last four minutes."

"Hallo, Specksy," shouted Claude, as he came rushing down the yard with Dan Dockery's hat.

"Come here, Claude," said Mr. Russel, banishing, with an effort, a smile.

Claude's pace tapered into a shamble and he advanced with the presentiment that he was to be called to order.

"It is great fun running off with boys' hats," observed the prefect.

"Yes, sir: I enjoy it pretty well."

"Of course, or you wouldn't do it. You like racing about like a mad colt."

"Yes, sir."

"Give me that hat."

"It's mine, sir," said Dan Dockery, coming up out of breath.

"Take it, Dan. How do you like to have people running off with your hat?"

As a matter of fact Dan had been meditating dire revenge upon Claude, but he was a kind-hearted boy and, now that the prefect was taking a hand in the matter, feared that he might bring Claude into trouble.

"Oh, I can stand it, sir, all right. Claude's a good fellow."

Claude gave Dan a grateful look.

"Yes, but you're willing to stand more than some boys," commented the prefect. "See here, Claude," he added with an air of severity, "if you go racing away with any more hats I'm going to have it out with you."

"I'll stop, sir." And Claude meant what he said.

Mr. Russel's good-natured air returned at once.

"Now suppose you jump against Dan Dockery, Claude; he's the best jumper under fourteen in the yard. Can you jump?"

"I like it better than running, sir," answered Claude, brightening up under the easy sympathy of the prefect.

"I thought so," said Mr. Russel, surveying the sturdy little fellow. "And I'm afraid that Dan has met his match at last."

"What'll you bet?" asked Dan with a grin.

He was a slim lad with black hair, dark roguish eyes, a slightly freckled complexion and an honest face.

Mr. Russel laughed. "I've got an orange in my pocket, and I'll give it to the best man."

"Will you go halves with me, Dan?" asked Charlie Pierson.

"Wait till I win, Charlie. Is it to be a running jump, sir?"

"What do you say, Claude?"

"It's all the same to me, sir," answered Claude, who was now tempting Frank Elmwood to spar.

"Well, let it be a running jump. Dan, you go first. Here now is the line." And the prefect marked a line upon the ground. A number of boys were now interested spectators.

Dan moved back some twelve yards and, coming forward at a swift gait, rose lightly into the air.

"Good!"

"First rate, Dan."

"You never did better." Dan's effort pleased all.

Claude marked the distance with his eye and said: "I can beat that."

There was a general laugh from the crowd. But the sharper-witted perceived at once that the newcomer was not boasting, for he had spoken with an air of conviction.

Claude walked back a few feet, took three strides, and leaped into the air.

"Whew!" came the chorus: for without apparent effort this youngster had passed eight inches beyond the spot where Dan had alighted.

"That beats the small boys' record here," said Elmwood. "I never saw anything like it."

"Claude," said Mr. Russel solemnly, "take those springs out of your legs."

"I haven't got any springs in my legs," cried Claude seriously.

"Well, you have a pair under your feet then."

"Have I? Now you see," and the winner stooped and began untying his shoe strings. The boys laughed, and Claude joined in when he perceived on looking up that Mr. Russel had been joking him.

While these words were passing, several professors had joined the spectators, and Claude was compelled to jump over and over, till it became patent to all that Dan Dockery was no longer the champion long-distance jumper of the small boys.

Claude shared his orange with Dan, and both of them had a "good time" during class in consuming their respective portions while Mr. Grace was explaining a sum at the blackboard.

After dinner, Mr. Russel called Harry Archer.

"Harry, you're in need of a good player for the junior 'Highfliers,' aren't you?"

"Yes, sir: we've only eight men since we threw Jim Shallow out for kicking too much and not minding what I told him."

"Why don't you try Claude Lightfoot?"

"Do you think he can play, sir?"

"I don't know. But even if he can't play at all, I'm inclined to think that he'll pick up more in a month than most boys would in three years. He's a born athlete. He has a quick eye and a quick leg—and perfect command over every muscle in his body. What do you say, Rob?" he asked, turning to Collins.

"I think it would be worthwhile trying him. Here, I've got the League ball that belongs to the Poetry boys in my pocket now. Suppose we get him over here?" Harry ran off and quickly returned with Claude.

"Can you play baseball, Claude?" asked the prefect.

"I can bat, sir, but I haven't practiced much."

"Can't you throw?" inquired the captain of the Marquette Juniors.

"Throw! Of course I can. Just let me have that ball!"

Claude grasped the ball and gazed about the yard. "Specksy! Specksy!" he shouted, as his eye fell upon Frank, who was conversing with John Winter near the home plate of the college diamond.

Frank turned toward the group.

"Here—catch this!" and with an easy movement of the forearm Claude sent the ball almost on a line straight into Frank's hand.

"Why, that's gorgeous!" cried Harry. "Here we are in left field, and that throw would have thrown out a fellow running from third base home. And did you notice, Mr. Russel, how he threw? It was all with his forearm. He just seemed to give the ball a smart push. How do you do it, Claude?"

Claude was now hopping about with his eyes fixed in the air, endeavoring to judge a high fly which Frank had thrown for his benefit. He judged it so accurately that the ball came squarely into his hands, but rolled out before his fingers could close upon it.

"You see, I'm not much at catching. But I've never practiced. I don't know how I throw, but it comes easy."

"Can you curve?" continued the captain.

"I don't know; I never tried. How is it done?"

"Get Elmwood to teach him," suggested Mr. Russel, "and you've secured a great pitcher. Look at his fingers—they are strong, and he can twist them around any ball. If he can put on a little curve and combine it with his speed, you'll have the best Junior nine that ever represented our college."

And then and there Claude became a member of the club.

But matters did not go so well with him in the classroom. He was frequently out of order, and, I am bound to say, sometimes inexcusably so. While some of his antics were quite involuntary, others were a deliberate yielding to temptation. He really gave Mr. Grace a deal of annoyance. How boys could wriggle so, Mr. Grace could not understand. At the end of the school day Claude was scolded, and he certainly deserved it.

But the scolding, earnestly and conscientiously given as it was, failed to impress him as it should have impressed him.

He was not able to analyze his feelings: but he felt obscurely that Mr. Grace was not in sympathy with him. He respected his professor; he loved Mr. Russel.

"What a troublesome boy! I wonder how his parents bear with him at home," was the inward comment of Mr. Grace, as Claude with flying heels rushed from the yard intent upon making the convent school in time to catch Kate.

"That's a splendid little fellow," soliloquized Mr. Russel. "He's healthy and happy and bright, and I hope a few years may make him wise."

Chapter V

IN WHICH THE READER OBTAINS A GLIMPSE OF CLAUDE AND KATE AT HOME

MR. Grace was under the impression, therefore, that Claude created trouble at home as he did in the classroom. Mr. Grace was mistaken. Indeed, it is sometimes very difficult to judge of a boy's home life by his conduct at school. The quiet, "nice" boy at school, in whose mouth butter is not supposed to melt, makes up, it may be, for his good conduct on more familiar ground. He gives his younger brothers and sisters no rest, and causes the servants of the house untold miseries. His parents wonder when they receive his school report and learn that he is a model boy. They try to believe it, too.

The harum-scarum of the classroom goes home and, once he has crossed the threshold, becomes a lamb. He runs errands for his mother, plays with little sister, and, when evening comes, buries himself in a tale of adventure. There is such a thing as the law of compensation.

Claude's home life was almost ideal. Let us follow him for one afternoon and evening.

On entering the house, his first care was to salute his mother, a delicate lady whose faded face gave more than a hint of the beauty that had once been hers. She had been an invalid for some years, and, not without a fond mother's regret, had intrusted Claude to Kate's care. Thus Kate at the age of fourteen had become Claude's little mother.

Mrs. Lightfoot's pale cheek flushed as Claude came tripping in and, without giving her time to rise from the sofa, kissed her heartily three distinct times. Then putting his arm around her neck, Claude ran through his second day's adventure at school. No wonder he was animated in his narrative: the fond eyes that looked into his would have inspired the most sluggish of tongues. Before he had completed his account, Kate, having changed her school dress for what she called her "playing gown," entered bright and rosy, and, taking her place on the other side of Mama, and with her arm about Mama's neck, the three chatted on unrestrainedly for some minutes. There was much love; there were no secrets.

"Well, Claude," said Kate after a glance at her watch, "we mustn't stay too long with Mama, or the doctor will keep us out entirely. Come on now for our game of lawn tennis."

Taking an affectionate farewell, brother and sister hurried away, Kate to secure the rackets, and Claude, whose appetite was perennial, to coax the cook into giving him a few cakes.

Kate in her white playing gown moved about with an ease and freedom surprising in a girl and played a game which few boys of her age could surpass. But Claude was a master. He skipped about with a never-failing command of his motions and handled his racket equally well with right or left hand. In each game he gave Kate thirty to begin on and, even thus handicapped, won the set after a long contest. It was a pretty sight, these two bright-eyed, rose-flushed children, as they moved about with never-failing agility and grace, while their laughter, unrestrained yet not harsh, rippled into music on the soft evening breeze.

Claude and Kate, when there were other players at hand, always played as partners; and they had yet to taste defeat.

After the match, the brother retired to the bathroom to enjoy his daily splash. This child of light and air had learned very early in life to love the cooling waters and, not without some natural repugnance, had become reconciled to the lavish use of soap.

Claude's reappearance from the bathroom was the signal for supper. Mr. Lightfoot, who had arrived from his law office toward the close of the lawn tennis set, presided. He was a hearty gentleman on this side of the prime of life, kind and considerate toward his children and tender to his invalid wife.

He had one hobby, and that was an offshoot of his patriotism. On arriving in the "States," he had been taken with the American people and with American institutions. This was very natural, and as it should be. But Mr. Lightfoot made his Americanism a convenient peg to hang his prejudices upon.

Whatever suited his whims he styled American; whatever ran counter to them was un-American. The Stars and Stripes entered largely into his conversation, and some of his Milwaukee friends tell a story of his refusing to allow in his house a picture of Columbus taking possession of the newly found country because the standard represented in the scene was not the American flag. The story, of course, was made up: but it shows how Mr. Lightfoot was regarded by his American friends.

Mr. Lightfoot had taken it into his head that the public schools were an American "institution." In the matter of parochial and Catholic schools, he was rather difficult, and it was only after long overtures and much diplomacy and constant tact that Mrs. Lightfoot had succeeded in persuading him to allow Claude to go to Milwaukee College. There had been no trouble, however, concerning Kate's going to the convent school. With all his prejudices, Mr. Lightfoot could not bring himself to send Kate to an "institution" where the co-educational system obtained.

During supper Mr. Lightfoot questioned Claude closely.

"Was there an American flag in your classroom, Claude?"

"I didn't notice, sir."

"Didn't you see any American flags at school?"

"No, Papa."

"And did you hear any of the professors talking about our government?"

"No sir: they asked me how I could jump; and they made me jump for them till I was tired. And one of 'em gave me an orange; he's a nice man."

Mr. Lightfoot went on with his questions, but failed to discover that the faculty was an enemy of our government or that the teachers were opposed to republican institutions. But he was not satisfied.

It was twilight when they arose from supper, and Claude, followed by Kate, went to his room to prepare his lessons for the following day.

The method of these two was certainly unique. Kate opened the Latin grammar, and Claude his pocketknife, with which he at once began to whittle.

"Now," said Kate, "let's hear you repeat the first and second declensions which we learned yesterday."

Whittling energetically, Claude, not stopping to pause or think, gave cases, endings and genders, without a single omission.

"Very good, Claude. Now listen: in the third declension the genitive ends in *is*; the nominative has all sorts of endings—example: *leo, leonis, leoni, leonem, leo, leone.*"

Kate paused. Apparently absorbed in his manual task, Claude repeated her words exactly as she had spoken them.

"Now for the plural—*leones, leonum, leonibus, leones, leones, leonibus.*"

There was a twinkle in Claude's eye as he began: "*Leonibus, leones, leones, leonibus, leonum, leones.*"

Oh, Claude, where's your memory! That was all wrong."

"No, it wasn't!" retorted Claude.

"Yes, it was. You began with *leonibus* and the nominative is *leones.*"

"Kit, I've caught you!" cried Claude, jumping to his feet and hopping about, while brandishing his knife and the bit of wood; "I said it *backward.*"

Kate laughed and owned herself outwitted. Within five minutes, the playful youth had mastered the third and fourth declensions, saying them backward or forward with equal readiness. From his first school days, he had done nearly all his studying by listening: his memory, naturally good, had become so sharpened by this exercise that he could repeat after one hearing any paragraph that Kate pronounced. The little romp was too impatient, too restless, too full of animal life to put himself down to hard study; and his sister's help, while cultivating his memory, did not succeed in adequately developing his understanding. Here was another of Claude's flaws. He trusted to the nimbleness of his wits rather than to their labor, and Kate found it impossible to make her brother settle down to severe duty.

They next took up United States History, and Kate after reading a paragraph gravely listened to Claude as one listens to a perfect echo. Before this lesson was quite disposed of, Claude betrayed signs of flagging attention. His eyes grew heavy, and he put his hands before his mouth several times to suppress a yawn. Like the birds of day, Claude grew quiet and sedate with the darkness. All his animation went to rest with the dying of the twilight.

"Let's say prayers, Kit," he said, when he had stumbled through the last few lines of the history lesson. "I can get up my examples in the morning."

Kneeling together upon the carpet, the two recited the Our Father, the Hail Mary and the acts of Faith, Hope and Charity. The restless boy appeared now in quite another character; with his hands folded and his eyes fixed on the crucifix above his bed, his whole attitude showed faith and devotion, while his sister looked like one of those sweet virgins whose lives are the glory of the Church.

Together had these two recited their prayers since the little lips were able to lisp in unison.

"God bless Papa and Mama," they went on, "and make me a good ——"

"Boy," said Claude.

"Girl," said Kate.

"Lord have mercy on brother Willie and all the suffering souls in Purgatory."

"Lord make me a good boy," continued Claude alone, "and prepare my heart to make a good First Communion."

Then after adding a prayer to their Mother Mary for perfect purity of soul and body, and making the Sign of the Cross, both arose, whereupon Kate slipped out, leaving Claude alone.

Fifteen minutes later, laying aside her own textbook, she crept softly in. It was her habit to return every night, and if Claude were sleeping, as was generally the case, she kissed his upturned cheek and returned to her books. If he were awake, she would seat herself beside him and receive such confidences as Claude had not the courage to tell her of in the glare of day. Then patting the little cheek or stroking the soft sunny hair, she would soothe her brother into slumber.

And later in the night, the invalid mother would enter—Claude knew nothing of this—and falling upon her knees she would pray long and devoutly for her little darling and, gazing into his face, would think of that other little one who had been taken from her in the first flush of radiant childhood. Who dares say that a Christian mother's grief for the loss of a little child is an unalloyed bitterness? It lifts the mother's heart to another and brighter world, and amid the heat and dust and grime of this life, she carries about with her a remembrance which links her sympathies and her longings with the beautiful land beyond, where the angel face of the departed shines down on her in unchangeable purity, radiant joy and undying love.

Chapter VI

*IN WHICH CLAUDE LOSES HIS TEMPER AND PUTS
HIMSELF DECIDEDLY IN THE WRONG*

THE first, second and third weeks of his
new life passed quite happily for little
Claude. In the yard he flitted about gay as
a sunbeam, and in the classroom, while giving full satisfaction in his recitations, he contrived, ably assisted by Mr. Grace, to *suppress*
himself, if I may use the expression, to the
required standard of discipline, with now
and then a startling failure.

It was hard for him to refrain from pinch-
ing any fat boy who came within his reach;
it was impossible for him to sit quiet when
anyone answered wrong, and in his zeal
to have the question answered rapidly he
would jump to his feet, dance half-way up
the room, while exclaiming in a blaze of
excitement, "Ask me, Mr. Grace!" He generally resumed his seat in a wilted condition. Despite his heroic efforts to keep
within bounds, he sorely dissatisfied his
professor, who, however, having discovered
early that Claude and himself could not
understand each other, had refrained from
speaking out his mind. So Claude flattered

himself that he was doing excellently.

Such too was the opinion of Father Maynard, who had charge of the First Communion class. He was deeply impressed with
the fair, flushed, bright-eyed face, so full of
interest, so clearly expressing the desire of
its owner to know and have at command
everything that bore upon the Catechism.
For, owing in great part to Kate's sweet influence, Claude had thrown his whole soul into
the work of preparation; and during the hour
devoted to Christian doctrine, he was a model
in conduct, on the one hand, and, on the
other, could repeat word for word not only
the answers but even the questions as they
stood in the book.

Many and many a time did Kate and
Claude discuss the coming of the great day.
It was the topic of their sweetest moments.
The last week of preparation had come, and
as Claude on Monday morning tripped lightly
to school, he little knew the troubles and
annoyances that were to try his very soul.

Besides the prospect of the coming day,
Claude had other cheering anticipations. To
begin with, under the skillful and eager train-
ing of Frank Elmwood, he had easily succeeded in getting the "in" and "out" curve.
Steady practice at noontime for half an hour

each day had given him so remarkable a command of the ball that he could put it over the base, and high or low, almost at will. The captain of the Highfliers was delighted with his progress and gave it out as his opinion that Claude, who had never yet pitched in a match game, was certainly the best small-boy pitcher, so far as he knew, in the city of Milwaukee: and to show that he was willing to stand by this opinion, he had challenged the "Rockaway" club of the East Side to a game on the coming Wednesday, with Claude "in the box." You may be sure that Claude looked forward to that afternoon with eagerness. He was by no means a timid boy, and was willing to stand up before the stoutest set of youngsters that ever shouldered the "willow."

In the next place, Claude was on this very day to buy for himself the finest boy's baseball bat that he had ever laid eyes on. It was a "Wagon Tongue," symmetrically fashioned, which had been resting for some time in a bundle of bats on sale at a certain notion store near the college. Claude had in passing noticed it, paused and, with permission of the shopkeeper, taken it out of the bundle and examined it. Now in the line of athletics, Claude possessed excellent judgment; and as he swung the bat at an imaginary ball, he was convinced that this particular bat was made for him.

"How much is it, Mister?"

"Seventy-five cents."

"Whew!" said Claude, taking a nickel out of his pocket and looking at it ruefully. "Won't you trust me, Mister? I'll give you five cents down and pay you the rest when I grow up."

Claude seldom left the house without ten or twenty cents in his pocket, and he never returned with anything. His mother, while grudging him nothing, did not consider it prudent for her child to carry a large sum.

"Cash sales here, Johnny," said the proprietor shortly.

"Well, Mister, won't you keep it for me?"

"I'll keep it till I get a buyer," answered the amiable merchant.

Claude told his sister of the occurrence that very afternoon, and on this Monday morning, Kate, who had been saving up for a week, handed her pet the required seventy-five cents. Then Kate, who had been on the point of starting off for school, was obliged to go back and readjust her toilet, and Claude's demonstrations of gratitude were within a little of bringing her late for class.

So Claude on this particular Monday morning was blithe as a bird in the first joyousness of spring. He carried his blithesomeness into class and, before noontime, received notice to copy twenty-five lines of his history and not to play after lunchtime till the lines were finished. Poor Claude! His bat, the only, the newly bought, was awaiting him; the boys were to play "rounds" immediately after lunch, and he had counted upon testing it in that one game. He had thought to hurry through his lunch, to be first in the yard, and, as soon as any small boy should appear, to shout, "Rounds! Innings!" The other small boy would shout in return, "Another!" and, as being first to bat, Claude would have an excellent chance of proving all the good qualities of his new acquisition. But now, what was he to do? Oh, yes: he could forego his lunch and write the lines during that time.

And this Claude did. He worked with unwonted celerity, finished his lines in a few minutes and dashed into the yard. Hurrah! Not a boy had appeared. He looked about for Mr. Grace, that he might give in his lines, but Mr. Grace was not to be seen.

"Rounds! Innings!" he shouted as Dan Dockery emerged from the lunchroom.

"Another!" screamed Dan.

"Catch!" called Pierson.

"Keep my place for me, Dan, while I go into the reading room and get my bat," panted Claude.

"All right," answered Dan.

Claude returned presently, breathless with excitement and aglow with pleasurable anticipation. By this time several boys were coming out, and pitch, first base, second base, third base, short-stop and left field were quickly claimed.

The time had at length come, and in an ecstasy of motion, Claude, bat in hand, dashed down the yard to take his position as batsman at the home plate.

"Claude," came a clear, distinct, baritone voice.

"Claude, Claude!" shouted a number of boys, "Mr. Grace wants you."

"All right; wait for me, fellows: I've just got to hand him some lines."

And Claude, anxious not to lose his place in the game, came running toward Mr. Grace, who was standing outside the storm door, and, as he ran, fumbled in his breeches pocket for the copy he had made.

He found it as he gained Mr. Grace's side and, forgetting, in the excitement of the moment, to remove his cap, handed the paper to his teacher.

"There it is, Mr. Grace, every word. I wanted to give it to you as soon as I finished it, but you weren't in the yard."

Then Claude turned and took three rapid springs.

"Claude! Come back."

Poor Claude winced and obeyed. He glanced wistfully at the bat in his hand—a glance that would have moved the heart of anyone who knew what a real American boy feels on the subject of baseball.

"The fellows are going to begin to play," said Claude, "and it's my turn at the bat."

"Business before pleasure, Claude."

Ah me! Some of these axioms can be so cruel.

"When did you write this?" continued Mr. Grace, very slowly, very deliberately, who, never having played ball in his life, and having nothing of the dramatic faculty, as I have already stated, was not at all moved by Claude's signs of haste.

"During lunch," said Claude, noticing with a sinking at the heart that Dan Dockery was at the bat.

"That was not the right time, Claude. I didn't want to deprive you of your lunch. Little boys should eat regularly."

"May I go, sir?" entreated Claude, almost sobbing, as he perceived that the players were discussing the question of putting another batsman in his place.

"No, go down to the lunchroom and eat your lunch." The clear, serene, slow accents in which Mr. Grace spoke were maddening in their utter lack of sympathy.

"I won't," burst forth Claude on the spur of the moment, his eyes flashing with anger. And then he could have bitten his tongue off. Oh, the pity of it! Here within a few days of his First Communion he had been impudent and defiant to a religious.

Oh, the pity of it, gentle reader, that with so much goodness and purity of intention we poor mortals go on maddening and worrying one another and crossing each other's lives in lines that lead to such ugly collisions. Mr. Grace had, unwittingly indeed, been really cruel to the child; he had tortured the lad into impudence. And yet Mr. Grace to this day, I dare assert, does not know that he had acted cruelly. He intended to be kind; he pitied the little fellow going about without his lunch, and in his kindness of suggestion had met with a flat, "I won't."

Claude would have apologized in the same breath, but, overcome by horror, shame and vexation, his voice broke, so that he could not trust it, and it was all he could do to keep back the tears.

"Claude! I am astonished at you. Go over there by the turning pole, and stay there till the first bell rings." And deeply hurt, Mr. Grace walked away.

Poor Claude! It was an affair of a baseball bat, but it was one of the great sorrows of his childhood.

He obeyed this time—but apologize? No: never. He had said, "I won't," and now he wasn't sorry. Mr. Grace was mean—yes, mean.

Now Mr. Grace was not mean. He was good and kind according to his lights: but they were half-lights. Yet we can pardon Claude for his misjudgment.

Presently Mr. Grace bethought him of the fact that Claude still needed his lunch, and in all kindness of heart he walked over toward the culprit to release him and send him to the lunchroom. But he approached Claude just as the waves of passion were surging highest in his bosom, and Claude, with a glare of dislike and defiance fixed full on Mr. Grace's face, deliberately turned his back on the prefect.

"What a rude boy!" he commented interiorly. "I see it will not be prudent for me to go near him now, for if I do, he'll surely give me more impudence."

Frank Elmwood came by.

"What's the matter, Claude?"

But Claude, his bosom still heaving, rubbed his hand over his eyes and made no answer.

The evening hours of class passed gloomily for our poor little friend, and Kate was driven to do all the talking on the way home.

After Claude had gone to bed, Kate entered to give him the good-night kiss. He was awake.

"Sit down, Kit, by my side; I've an awful story to tell you."

And Claude told her all.

Kate said very little, but in those tender feminine ways which good and tactful women employ so well, she soothed the wounded heart and banished from Claude every touch of unkind feeling.

"Now, my dear, you'll apologize to Mr. Grace in the morning."

"Yes, Kit; I've been bad. But it was hard."

"So it was, dear; but we'll begin all over, shall we not?"

"Yes, Kit."

Yes: Claude had been bad; his rudeness to Mr. Grace was very wrong. But who of us would hesitate to accept his chance for

Heaven had he died that night? The poor boy fell asleep with an act of contrition on his lips and great resolves in his heart.

Chapter VII

IN WHICH CLAUDE ASTONISHES HIS EXAMINERS IN CATECHISM AND HARRY ARCHER IN MATTERS OF BASEBALL

ON Monday Claude had passed through the storm; on Tuesday he basked in the sunshine. The class of First Communion, having completed the Catechism, was to be examined on this day by a board consisting of the president, vice president and a professor of the faculty. It was to be a contest as well as an examination; for upon its result was to depend the awarding of two prizes, the first being a handsome pocket edition of the New Testament, and the second a morocco-bound Thomas à Kempis.

Owing mainly to Claude, the examination went on briskly. As Dan Dockery put it, Claude was first, and the others were nowhere.

At the end of the set examination, the president began to quiz the class.

"Here's a question," he said, "that isn't in your Catechism exactly as I put it; but it's quite easy. Who has the right of giving the Holy Eucharist?"

"A priest!" cried several.

"Could a religious not in Holy Orders give it?"

"No, sir."

"Could a living saint, supposing he were not a priest, touch the Consecrated Host?"

"No, sir."

"Why is the Church so strict in this matter?"

There was a silence: the boys looked at each other at first, then, as if by common consent, fixed their eyes on Claude.

"I think, Father," said Claude, "that it's because of the great reverence which we should show to Our Lord."

"And you are quite right, Claude: the Church hedges the Holy Eucharist about with all manner of restrictions for fear lest men through familiarity should lose their reverence. However, can any of you think of an instance where even a layman might give Holy Communion?"

The faces of all the boys, save Claude's,

became blank; Claude's brow furrowed with lines.

"What do you say, Claude?"

"I'm thinking, Father."

"Suppose a man were dying, and no priest could be got, and suppose that the Blessed Eucharist were at hand: might a layman give it to the dying man?"

"I think he might, sir, in that case."

"Why, Claude?"

"Because there's no other chance of the dying man's getting Communion; and besides, as Father Maynard says, the Sacraments are all for the good of the people."

"You are right, Claude, but the case is so extreme that practically it comes to nothing. Whenever there's any question about the Holy Eucharist, it can be answered if we keep in mind that we owe it the greatest love on the one hand, and on the other the deepest reverence."

"That brings another question to my mind," broke in the vice president. "You all know how extremely strict the Church is in insisting on a total fast from midnight for those who are to communicate. The reason for this exceeding strictness is the high reverence we owe our Divine Lord. Now, is it ever allowed for a person to receive Holy Communion who has broken the fast?"

"Yes, sir," answered Dan Dockery; "anyone who is dying may receive the Holy Eucharist whether he's fasting or not."

"Correct. But who can give me another case where the law of fasting ceases to bind?"

"Oh, I know, sir!" cried Claude, springing to his feet, and then dropping back in confusion at his forwardness. "A person not fasting could receive Holy Communion, even if there weren't a priest at hand to give it, in order to save it from being insulted by bad men or by wicked soldiers in time of war."

"Where did you learn that?" asked the astonished vice president, while his fellow examiners exchanged glances of surprise.

"My sister read it to me out of a book, sir."

"You have answered well; out of reverence, we fast before going to Communion; out of reverence, only those in Holy Orders may touch the sacred Host—but again, out of love for the honor of Our Lord, fasting and all such rules may, should an extreme occasion arise, be done away with."

Then the quizzing went on. I have here set down but two of the questions with their answers, first to show how quick and thorough Claude was, secondly because, as the reader shall find out later, they will throw much light on Claude's subsequent history.

"Father Maynard," said the president immediately after the examination, "I congratulate you on the thorough preparation you have given all your boys; but as for that little cricket, I never saw anything like it. Indeed, I couldn't imagine a boy of his years better prepared."

"I can hardly claim any credit for that: some of Claude's knowledge seems to be infused."

He did not know that Kate "infused" it.

At noontime Claude was in his element as he stepped up to the home plate with his bat.

"Throw the ball with all your might!" he piped to the pitcher.

It came straight and swift; there was a sharp crack, and Claude ran for first base while the ball shot into the air and struck the college building far over the left fielder's head. When his turn came again, he sent the ball straight over second base. Next he drove a long fly into right field—and then Claude was happy: the bat had come up to his expectations, for not only could he hit hard with it, but he could place the ball in any field he chose.

Few small boys think of attempting scientific batting. They strike as hard as they can and are glad if they succeed in hitting the ball at all. But Claude, with his singularly steady eye and wondrous flexibility of muscle, was never haunted with the fear of striking out. There was no question as to his hitting or not hitting the ball; therefore, he could pay attention to the placing of his hits. He gave promise of becoming a marvellous batter.

"Where are you going after school, Claude?" asked Harry Archer.

"To the East Side to take my sister home from school."

"I wanted to have a talk with you about tomorrow's game."

"Well, why not walk along with me?"

Harry scratched his head.

"I could go with you as far as the State Street bridge."

"All right. I shall wait for you here after class."

"Now," began Harry, running his arm through Claude's that afternoon as the boys with books and satchels came trooping into the yard, "I want to tell you about the Rockaway club. They're the crack small boys' nine of the East Side, and they haven't lost a game this season."

"Didn't they ever play our nine?"

"Yes: last year, and they won three straight from us. Two of the games were pretty close, but in the last game they beat us 12 to 3."

"Were our fellows afraid of them?"

"No; but the Rockaways had strengthened their nine, ours was the same. Now, of course, they don't want to break their record by letting us beat them this year; and some of our college fellows from the East Side have been blowing about your pitching so that they've become terribly worked up. And now they are trying to steal a march on us."

"How's that?"

"They've been scouring the city for undersized good players. You know the agreement between us is that all players on either side must be under fifteen. Well, they've got hold of three sawed-offs, stumpy little chaps, and one of them is sixteen, and the other two fifteen. All three are splendid players, and they're going to be put in the infield."

"How did you hear about it, Harry?"

"Oh, I keep my eyes open; and besides, I get Frank Elmwood to look out for me. And now I'm thinking of getting in two undersized fellows from the South Side to strengthen our nine, too."

"Two wrongs don't make a right," said Claude with a laugh.

Archer thought for a moment.

"That's so; let's show our pluck anyhow. Even as it is, we can beat 'em if we use our heads. But some of them are awful [awesome] batters: I've been following them up every game they played this spring, and I tell you there are three or four of them, if they get the ball where they want it, will send it to glory every time."

"If I only knew the kind of balls they wanted," sighed Claude.

"Oh, I can fix that," said Harry eagerly. "I know the weak and strong batting points of every fellow on the regular nine, and I've got Elmwood to find out about the three outsiders. Tonight, I'll write down their names and put after each the kind of ball they can hit and the kind they can't. It'll be hard work for me. But it'll be just as hard for you to learn it by heart."

Claude smiled.

"I can save you all that trouble, Harry. Just name your boys and tell me all you know about them."

"You can't remember it all. You'll get names and everything else mixed up."

"Try me," said Claude.

Then Harry started out, and talked, talked, talked, in one continuous flow of baseball slang, not even pausing when the bridge was reached. He seemed to have forgotten his intention, for on he went across the river, giving the results of his close and long-continued observations. It was only when they had gone six squares further east that he came to a pause.

"Gracious!" he added after catching his breath, "that was the longest speech I ever made. But of course you can't remember it."

"Listen," said Claude.

And he did listen, with distended eyes and open mouth, for Claude repeated what he had heard almost word for word and without omitting a single material point.

"My goodness!" gasped Harry. "How do you do it?"

"Ask my sister."

"But how long can you remember it?"

"For two or three days, even if I were not to think of it again. But I'll go over it tonight once more, Harry, and you'll see tomorrow that I haven't forgotten."

Suddenly Harry turned and fled: the girls were just coming out of the convent.

Chapter VIII

*IN WHICH CLAUDE PITCHES AGAINST THE ROCK-
AWAYS AND MEETS WITH ANOTHER TRIAL*

"**P**LAY ball!" called the umpire, and
Sniderjohn, a stunted youth, one of the
three outsiders, took his place at the bat.

Frank Elmwood had told Claude to give
him a high ball. But alas! Claude's fingers
slipped in the act of delivery—it was the
first time he had ever pitched in a real contest—and he sent the ball straight over the
plate, and not quite waist high. O'Neil in
center field had a hard run to catch up with
the long line ball that Sniderjohn knocked,
and when he had returned it to the infield,
the heavy batsman was standing on third
base.

The Highfliers were startled and uneasy.
Claude, perhaps, was to turn out an "exploded
phenomenon."

As Gardner waited at the plate (he was
the second of the outsiders), a great stillness came over all, and Claude felt that he
was in danger of becoming nervous.

The college boys, some eighty or ninety in
attendance, had nothing to say.

"Knock a home run, Gardner!" broke in

Sniderjohn. "That pitcher is a pie."

"Am I?" cried Claude angrily.

Then he turned and faced the batter with all his nervousness gone, the coolest, most fearless boy on the field.

"This is the fellow who doesn't want an in-curve," he whispered to himself.

"One strike," called the umpire, as the ball whirled in and over the plate.

"Two strikes," he said, as the next ball was batted at vainly by Gardner.

Then waist-high, straight over the base and swift, came the third ball, and before the batter had made up his mind to strike, the ball was in the hands of Archer, Claude's catcher.

The friends of the Rockaways applauded when Williams advanced to the plate. He was the third outsider and, according to Elmwood, was the best batter on the team.

Archer pulled up one of his stockings; that meant, "Give this man his base on balls."

"Four balls, take your base," said the umpire presently.

O'Brien, the next batter, knocked a slow grounder to the shortstop. It was what is called a "good sacrifice hit"; for Sniderjohn was nearly home before the shortstop, who had been playing deep, could put his hands on it. Allowing Sniderjohn to score, he threw O'Brien out at first. Jones struck out, and the Highfliers came in with cheerful faces. Claude had, after all, come up to their expectations.

Dan Dockery was their first batsman. He was not a powerful hitter, but he had a knack of getting his base by hook or by crook, in the innocent sense of this phrase; and once on base the chances were in favor of his getting around, for he was both quick and sure-footed.

The second ball pitched came straight at Dan's ribs. Covering his side with his arm, he stepped back with measured deliberation just as the ball was upon him. It struck him full on the arm.

"Take your base," said the umpire.

"You did that a-purpose," shouted pitcher Snyder indignantly.

"Did what?" laughed Dan, as he trotted down to first. "I thought you did it."

Archer, who had now stepped up to the plate, suppressed a grin: he knew Dan's tricks.

The captain of the Juniors made a mistake in judgment, for he struck at a "drop" ball which came below his knee. It rolled toward first. But Dan was safe on second before the first baseman could touch his bag.

When Claude faced the pitcher, he received a rousing greeting from the college boys. His cheeks flushed with pleasure.

Claude wanted a high ball, and the second one pitched was just an inch or two above his shoulder. His bat met it full and square; the ball went on a line over the third baseman's head, bounded high over the left fielder, and before it was returned to the diamond, Dockery had scored and Claude stood on third base.

"I say, Sniderjohn," called out Frank Elmwood, "how's your pie?"

Pierson knocked a fly to short right field. Darby, the fielder of that position, caught it after a lively run. Then Claude, who had kept one foot on third base till the ball touched Darby's hands, dashed for home. Darby threw the ball in, but Claude, the fleet of foot, had beaten it. Walter Collins, Rob's younger brother, went out on a foul fly to the first baseman, and the second inning began with the score 2 to 1 in favor of the Highfliers.

Darby struck out, and Healy followed his example. Phillips drove a swift grounder to Pierson, who fumbled it, then threw wide of the first baseman and thus allowed Phillips to reach third. Snyder knocked a fly to Walter Collins, and the Rockaways took the field.

In the Highfliers' half of the inning O'Neil made a base hit; but he was left on second, as the three following batsmen went out in one, two, three order.

Sniderjohn did not get the kind of a ball he wanted this time. He knocked a high fly to Collins, who caught it with ease.

Gardner took his base on balls. Williams hit the first ball and sent it straight and hard at Claude. Claude muffed it, but picking it up quickly, threw the runner out. O'Brien made three strikes, and Gardner was left on second.

Dan Dockery was easily retired on a grounder. Archer did not repeat his error of judgment. He struck the ball for two bases and stole third. Claude deliberately knocked a slow grounder between first and second base. He was thrown out, but Archer scored on this model sacrifice hit. Pierson did nothing at the bat, and the Juniors walked into the field with the score 3 to 1 in their favor. Claude now surpassed himself. Three batsmen retired, each with three strikes recorded against him.

And forthwith the Highfliers plucked up heart of grace. Walter Collins made a single. O'Neil advanced him to second on his out at first, and Drew sent the ball far into right field, bringing Collins home and reaching second base. Overbeck made first on a juggled ball, and Stein brought both home on a long fly which was misjudged by the center fielder. Dockery took his base on balls, Archer made a sacrifice hit after Dockery had stolen second, bringing in Stein; and with two out and Dockery on third, Claude came to the bat.

"Hit it for all you're worth—no sacrifice this time!" whispered Archer.

Claude gave a mighty swing of his bat as the third ball came curving in over the plate, and the center and left fielder both started out at full speed after the ball, which was rolling toward the boundary of the ball ground. It was a good three-base hit. Pierson made a neat single, and Claude scored. Collins was thrown out by the third baseman. Score at the end of fourth inning: 9 to 1 in favor of the Juniors.

Healy, Phillips and Snyder of the opposing nine were easily put out: the first on a fly to the second baseman, and the other two on easy grounders.

For the Highfliers, O'Neil and Drew made singles. O'Neil tallied on Overbeck's out at first. But Drew was left on third, as Stein struck out, and Dockery was retired on a foul to the third baseman. Score at the end of the fifth inning: 10 to 1 in favor of the Juniors.

The opposing players were now in very bad humor. They saw that with Claude in the box they could do very little. Sniderjohn, as he stepped to the bat, received a whispered communication from Healy, the captain of the Rockaways.

Harry Archer's quick ear caught the words: "If you get a chance, let the pitcher hit you."

Then Harry waved his left hand to Claude, which meant, "Pitch a swift, straight ball."

Claude obeyed.

"One strike." Sniderjohn stood like a statue.

"One ball!"

"Two balls!"

"Two strikes!" Still, Sniderjohn moved not a muscle. "Look out!" screamed Claude as the next ball came from his hand. But Sniderjohn moved not till the ball struck him squarely in the ribs. Then he gave a scream of pain and threw his bat savagely at Claude, who barely succeeded in dodging it.

"Did I hurt you?" cried Claude, running up to the home plate. "I didn't want to hit you."

For answer, Sniderjohn struck him a violent blow on the mouth. Claude never deliberately went into a fight, but it had been his constant habit to return any blow given him. I say "habit," for our reckless little friend had so often provoked his older companions by acts of thoughtlessness that the present situation was by no means new to him. The result was that Claude was frequently drawn into a bout with lads his superiors both in weight and strength. That mattered little to Claude; he knew not what physical fear was. With a flush of anger he raised his fist and was about to answer in kind when, with a sudden paling of the features, he checked himself and returned to his box.

"Goodness gracious," he reflected, "that was hard. But I hope it'll make up for my conduct to Mr. Grace."

Bravo, little Claude!

Frank Elmwood and Rob Collins did not take the matter so calmly.

"Bah! You wretched coward," cried Frank, advancing on Sniderjohn with flashing eyes. "I've a notion to rub your wretched ears into your wooden warehouse of a head."

"He nearly killed me," answered Sniderjohn.

"None of that, Sniderjohn!" broke in Archer. "It was your own fault! You wanted to be hit, and you got it in the ribs. Maybe I didn't hear your captain a-whispering to you."

"That's a lie!" said Sniderjohn.

"You'd better remember that you're talking to a gentleman," put in Rob Collins hotly, "which doesn't happen to you very often."

"Who are you?" roared Sniderjohn.

"No, thanks," answered Rob, "I'd prefer to get along without being introduced. But I say, Archer, this thing has gone far enough. That fellow's a fraud. He's sixteen if he's a day, and he doesn't belong to the East Side: he lives in the southern part of the city. Make their captain, Healy, stand up to his agreement. If you don't, I'll try to get my brother home. I don't care about his playing with a fellow like that."

Healy, who was something of a gentleman, though not remarkable for strength of character, gave in to Archer's demand: Sniderjohn slunk into the crowd, and the game proceeded. The substitute for Sniderjohn took first base. However, as he was thrown out in an attempt to steal second, nothing came of it. Gardner's fly was caught by the right fielder. Williams redeemed his waning reputation by making a two-base hit. He remained on second base as O'Brien struck out.

The Juniors started their half of the inning very well. Archer made a safe hit, stole second and easily made third on the grounder which Claude knocked into the first baseman's hands. Pierson was the second out on a long fly to center field, on which Archer scored. Collins struck out. Score at the end of the sixth inning: 11 to 1.

Claude was standing in the pitcher's box and about to begin the seventh inning when he suddenly dropped the ball and, calling time, ran toward the backstop. All turned their eyes in that direction and saw Sniderjohn flying down the street with Claude's bat. But Claude had been so quick to discover this contemptible act of treachery that Sniderjohn, who was a poor runner in comparison with his pursuer, very shortly gave up the attempt at flight and, turning, swung the bat in rapid half circles about his face. Nothing daunted, Claude, with a quick dive, caught his adversary about the feet and brought him suddenly to the ground, receiving, as he did so, a sharp blow upon his right leg.

Sniderjohn was making another attempt to strike this little boy with the bat when Frank Elmwood, who had at once rushed to the scene of action, caught him by the neck and, swinging him to his feet, shook him as a dog would shake a rat.

"Drop that bat!" he commanded.

And the bat was dropped.

"Now, sir, make yourself scarce or it will be the worse for you!" And as Frank spoke he released his hold.

Muttering some ugly words, Sniderjohn shambled away.

Claude had received an ugly blow, and it was several minutes before the game could be resumed.

Although his leg pained him not a little, he pitched with the same energy. It was now growing dark, and the batsmen struck out in one—two—three order.

Archer saw that Claude could not hold out for two more innings and asked the umpire to call the game on account of darkness.

Healy would have protested, ordinarily, but now he was so ashamed of Sniderjohn's conduct that he submitted without demur; and so the Highfliers left the field with a glorious victory over what had thus far been the invincible small boys' nine of Milwaukee.

Claude was hardly able to walk: his leg was swelling more and more each minute. Frank Elmwood and Rob Collins took him between them and, bracing him up firmly, brought him home.

But for all their merry words and sincere congratulations, they could bring no cheer to Claude's heart. On the morrow, the boys of the First Communion class were to begin a three days' retreat, and now he could scarcely move his leg, and his upper lip was sadly puffed out from Sniderjohn's cowardly blow. He feared—and as the event proved, not without reason—that he would be kept at home for at least two days, and of all days the two that were so important. Had it not been for the presence of his kind friends, Claude would have cried.

But where they failed to console, Kate succeeded. She listened that evening, as he lay in bed with his leg in bandages, to his account of the ball game.

"It was so good of you, dear," she said with her eyes beaming, "not to have returned that blow. Claude, you know how we're all so anxious about your temper. Mama was afraid only last year that it was going to be ungovernable."

"It's an awful bad one yet, Kit. If it weren't for my religion, I don't know what would become of me; and it's all owing to you, Kit, that I've improved the little I have."

"Well, dear, you have never told me anything that encourages me so much as the way you acted when that boy struck you."

"Is that so, Kit?" In the delighted energy with which he put this question, Claude jumped up in bed, only to fall back with a suppressed groan as a sharp pain shot through his leg.

"It is, dear; indeed it is. You remember the story of Pancratius and how he refused to return the blow? You thought he was a hero. Well, my dear, God helped you in much the same way as He helped him."

"Yes; but wasn't I just boiling over? I felt as if I could have given my life to return that blow."

"So much the better—you had more to conquer. Claude, my brother, I am sure that you will grow up to be a noble man."

"Thank you, Kit; and now I'm willing to stay in bed for two days. I'm glad I reminded you of Pancratius; but the boy that I love even more than him is the little chap who died taking care of the Blessed Sacrament. Kate, Tarcisius is my hero, and I so wish I were like him."

Then Kate and Claude said night prayers with swelling hearts.

Chapter IX

IN WHICH CLAUDE SPENDS TWO DAYS IN BED

IT was Claude's wont to awake with the early birds, spring from bed and begin the day in full flow of blithesomeness. But on Thursday morning he lay quite still, with his eyes fixed wistfully on the golden eastern sky. One day of imprisonment! Perhaps two days! Claude was appalled at the prospect.

"May I come in, dear?" whispered a soft voice outside.

"Come in, Kate. I'm so glad you're up."

Kate stooped to kiss Claude, and her fresh smiling face gave him comfort.

"I got up early to keep you company, Claude."

"You always do what's kindest."

"And besides, I have good news."

"Ah! I thought there was something coming, Kit; I could see it in your face. What is it?"

"Mama has given me permission to stay away from school to nurse you."

"Oh, Kit!" And Claude took her hand in so hearty a grasp that Kate could not refrain from wincing.

Shortly after the family breakfast, Mrs. Lightfoot entered.

"My poor little cripple!" she cried as she caught Claude in her arms. "You were tossing all night."

"How did you know that, Mama?" asked Claude in wonderment. He knew not the many hours of prayerful watches that had been passed beside his bed.

"Now, Kate," said the mother, ignoring her boy's question, "you might go to the college at once and tell Father Maynard of Claude's condition. Tell him that we shall have Claude up and about, please God, by Saturday morning; and ask him what we shall do during these two days. I will stay with Claude till you come back."

Kate went off at once.

"Claude, I spent a long time last night thinking about all you told me, and the more I thought, the more I was satisfied."

"I'm so glad, Mama."

"It has taken a great weight off my mind, dear. I have always trembled for your fiery temper. I know what a temper is and what it costs." Here Mrs. Lightfoot sighed. "But now, Claude, I see that you are on the way to breaking it. Mind, dear, you haven't conquered it yet. You may have trouble again on account of it, but I am sure that with God's grace you will conquer."

"And my First Communion will be sure to help me—don't you think so, Mama?"

"Undoubtedly; and, Claude, I hope that it will take a good deal of your giddiness out of you. You are so reckless, my dear; and I often think that if it weren't for your Angel Guardian's special care you would have been killed or maimed long ago."

"That's so," sighed Claude, "and I always like to pray to my Angel because I know he's been a good friend of mine. And St. Joseph has got me out of a heap of scrapes; he's good to me too. It's a fact, Mama; I am reckless. But then, you see, I don't have time to think. Now, yesterday, if I'd had any sense, I'd have waited for Rob Collins and Frank Elmwood to come up, and I'd have got my bat without having my leg smashed."

Mrs. Lightfoot was in better health than usual that morning, and she contrived, like the good mother that she was, to interest her darling boy and to spur him on in his honest endeavors.

Kate returned very shortly.

"Oh, Mama," she said, "you should have seen how concerned Father Maynard was about Claude. He said that Claude needn't fret, and that even if he couldn't come to the college on Saturday, it would be all right, because Claude is so well prepared already. He told me that I should give Claude a retreat in my own way," added Kate with a pleasant laugh, "and if by Saturday Claude were still unwell, he promised to come up here and hear his Confession."

"That Father Maynard," said Mr. Lightfoot gravely, who had entered the room after Kate, "is an American."

"He's a nice man, I can tell you," added Claude.

Mr. Lightfoot looked closely at his son.

"How do you feel, my boy?"

"First rate, Papa."

"I don't like that lip of yours. When my son makes his First Communion, I want him to look respectable. You must get that lip down to its proper size and have your legs in good walking order, or you'll have to stay at home next Sunday."

Claude grew very pale.

"You needn't fear, Claude," said Kate; "I'll nurse you night and day, if it's needful."

"That's right, Kate," said the father kindly. "And get him anything he wants. Don't spare anything. I love my boy too much to see him make his Communion in a discreditable condition."

Mr. Lightfoot looked upon a boy's First Communion as a public ceremony. His early schooling and his later readings had led him to attach too much importance, even in religious matters, to externals.

Perceiving Claude's dismay, he added a few kind words before setting out for his law office.

"Well," said Claude to his sister, "if I don't get well soon enough it serves me right."

"Why, dear?"

"For my ugly conduct to Mr. Grace. Kate, it was awful. When I turned my back on him, I knew it was wrong; and still I did it." And Claude sighed.

This small boy had a delicate conscience. He was thoughtless in the act, but very thoughtful in the retrospect. Many a word spoken or deed performed in mere lightness of heart had come back to him at night in memories charged with remorse. His preparation for Communion had, as is natural, increased the delicacy of his conscience—to such a degree, indeed, that he often saw sin where sin was not.

"Don't worry about that, dear," said Kate in her soothing tones. "God knows your heart, my brother, and He is as quick to raise us as we are to fall."

And Kate in her sweet, winning way went on to speak of God's goodness and mercy, bringing everything to bear upon the Sacrament of His love.

What with conversation, reading, the doctor's visit and a few games of checkers, the morning passed quickly and pleasantly.

In the afternoon Messrs. Grace and Russel called.

While Kate entertained Mr. Russel, Mr. Grace addressed himself to his pupil.

"It's very kind of you to come to *me,* sir," said Claude, gratefully.

"Not at all," answered Mr. Grace. "You mustn't think of that little scene we had, Claude. I was surprised, but it's all over."

"And besides that," said Claude, "I'm such a nuisance to you in class; but I'm doing my best, sir."

"And so am I, Claude. Sometimes I think that I'm too hard on some of you; but I can't see clearly where I am too severe. So, my boy, if it should happen that I should seem to be harsh with you, you must think that I'm doing my best; and whenever you annoy me, I'll try to think you are doing your best. Is it a bargain?"

And Mr. Grace's smile was very kind and his eye very soft as he looked down into the face of the patient. He was quite a different man when dealing with the sick and the suffering, and Claude now perceived for the first time that Mr. Grace had a tender heart.

"Yes, sir: I agree. I didn't think of it that way before."

"But I warn you, Claude, that my *trying* to think so may not be the same as my thinking so. I never could understand why some boys should be so boisterous."

Claude and Mr. Grace spoke with each other very freely; and before their conference had ended, Mr. Grace had said some very beautiful and very consoling things, which set Claude's soul into a warmer glow of desire for the coming Sunday. Mr. Grace's best teaching was done outside classroom and playground.

The visitors left the children very happy indeed, and the evening found the two entertaining Rob and Frank. Thanks to the kindness and love of so many, Claude's day, which in the forecast had promised so ill, turned out to be most happy. Frank, before leaving his little friend, handed him a package.

"Mr. Grace," he said, "asked me to give you this. I don't know what it is, but I hope it may give you pleasure."

Claude's eyes sparkled when he opened the packet and held up the picture of the little Roman child Tarcisius, his hands clasped tightly and hugging to his bosom the Christian Mysteries [the Blessed Sacrament] while facing undauntedly the savage rabble that was about to take the life of him who, happy child, enjoyed the sublime privilege of carrying in his tiny hands Him who was the Life indeed. Claude said, "God bless Mr. Grace" in his night prayers, and he put an amount of intensity into that little invocation. As for the picture of Tarcisius, Claude's hero, he could hardly let it out of sight for a moment. This was the first lively boy that Mr. Grace had ever really won, and in the winning, Tarcisius, beautiful little Saint, entered into the conquered one's life.

The next day passed quietly.

At last Saturday dawned, and with the dawn's flush upon his happy face arose Claude. He joined the boys in retreat, and in the afternoon made a General Confession of his whole life; then, blithe and happy, he left the College grounds to meet his heaviest cross—so cruel a cross that I have scarcely the heart to enter into the particulars.

Chapter X

IN WHICH CLAUDE MEETS WITH HIS CROSS

CLAUDE left the "Sign of the Blue Flag" in the highest of spirits. He could have danced and leaped all the way home. The genial proprietor, who really loved our little madcap, had chosen him a suit of clothes, neat, pretty and a perfect fit, for the great morning so near at hand. Claude would have carried the bundle himself, but his friend would not hear of it.

"You can trust me," he said, "to see that this package gets home before you. I wouldn't trust you with it, Claude: you'd be turning somersaults on it before you got across the bridge to Grand Avenue, and by the time you reached home your new suit wouldn't be fit to wear in a baseball game."

Claude laughed gayly, and trebling forth a cheery good-evening, hopped out of the store. People gazed at him with interest and pleasure as he moved along—and no wonder. A face at once so beautiful and so gay was a rare and charming sight. I said just now that Claude could have danced and leaped on his way: one thing restrained him. His right leg was still stiff and sore, and his doctor had warned him that any great exertion might cripple him for a week; so Claude limited his expressions of jubilation to hopping now and then upon his left foot and to snapping his fingers in the air.

He had gone two squares beyond the bridge when his happy, sunny face caught the attention of a lady in deep mourning. Her sad face lighted tenderly as she gazed upon the lad, and a look of wistfulness and infinite longing came into her eyes.

He caught her gaze and smiled. The lady with the strange pathos upon her features advanced to Claude and, bending down, said in trembling tones, "Permit me, my dear."

And she pinned a rosebud upon his lawn-tennis shirt, while Claude, awed by her face, watched her in wonder. Then the lady touched his forehead lightly with her lips and turned away with a sob to think of her own little boy who lay under the green grass out by the Soldiers' Home.

He ceased hopping for fully two squares. Then, as he went past the Public Library and found himself on that part of the Avenue where the residence portion begins, and where, in consequence, the streets are not so thronged, he broke into a merry song. Claude had a sweet voice, and in the fullness of his joy he sang with an abandon that gave his notes the freshness and spontaneity of a bird.

By and by he left the Avenue and, taking one of the by-streets, turned north. He had gone but half a square when a pair of hands were clapped rudely over his eyes, each of his arms was seized, and he was forced along whither he knew not.

Claude kicked and plunged wildly.

"Grab his legs," whispered the one whose hands were over Claude's eyes, in a voice that seemed familiar.

Claude gave a cry of pain, as one of his captors, in grasping him by the legs, bore heavily upon the part so lately injured. He said no more, for a hand was placed over his mouth. Although he could see nothing, he had already discovered that his assailants were three in number; secondly, that they were large boys; thirdly, that two of them were smoking cigars.

Presently he heard the sound of a door opening, and he could feel that they had passed in out of the open air and that his captors were carrying him up a flight of steps. A moment later, the hands were removed from his eyes, and turning, he found himself face to face with Worden.

Worden, it may be remarked, had been expelled from college two weeks previous, for reasons that were not given out to the students.

Claude had a quick eye and was a minute observer. He took in at a glance the fact that they were in the hayloft of the stable; that one half of the roomy loft was piled with hay, while the other half, where they were now grouped together, was bare, save for a few wisps of hay upon the floor, a three-pronged pitchfork, and, upon a shelf near the entrance to the loft, a coal-oil can, a curry comb and an empty candlestick. With his back to the door, a smile of triumph and malignity upon his face stood Worden, and on either side of him two callow youths with pimpled faces who were both puffing away at cigars.

The group thus fronting Innocence would have made an excellent study for the "Three Disgraces."

Their costume is not worth describing. Take the fashionable dress of the time, imagine that fashion carried to the point of extravagance, the colors to flashiness, and the picture is complete.

"Take care not to drop those cigars up here, fellows," said Worden in a low voice.

Claude heard the remark and treasured it up.

"Now, monkey, I've got you," he added, leering at his victim. "And I'm going to make you pay up for your impudence."

Claude said nothing; he had folded his arms and stood gazing steadily into Worden's eyes.

"Slap him over, Worden," said the longer-legged of the trio.

"Stick his head in the hay and hold him there for an hour," said the other.

Claude felt in his heart that his faults were "coming home to roost." In pure lightness of heart and thoughtlessness he had taken many liberties with Worden during the few weeks they had been together at school. Frank Elmwood and Rob Collins had warned him time and time again to keep clear of the bully, but he had not appreciated the advice. He had dared the lion, and now he stood face to face with him in his den.

"No," said Worden in answer to these suggestions, "we'll have some fun out of the monkey first, and then I'll fix him so's he'll remember me till he dies."

His face was very cruel as he spoke. Claude still said nothing. Without appearing to do so, he took note of everything within reach. There were sharp pains shooting through his injured leg, but he was too busy with contriving to give them thought. He noticed now that there was a buggy whip behind the door and that a large window at his side looked out upon the lawn below. The whip was beyond his reach; to jump from the window meant a broken limb at the very least. He said a prayer to St. Joseph for light, another to his Angel Guardian for protection.

And yet he was not terrified. Claude had come free of many a danger, had faced and escaped many a peril. His recklessness, it is scarcely any exaggeration to say, had brought him to such a habit of living that he might be said, in a certain sense, to carry his life in his hands. Horses had run away with him, vchicles had been within an ace of running over his body, men had chased him in anger— yet, in all his little experience, he had never been brought to such a pass as the present. But in such a crisis, to St. Joseph and his Angel had he ever confided his personal safety, and to his Angel and St. Joseph did he now look.

"Monkey," continued Worden, "perform some of your monkey tricks for us."

Claude still faced him in silence.

"Do you understand? Show us what you can do. Come on; you can begin with a hand-spring."

"I'll not," said Claude, checking as well as he could his rising anger.

"Is that the way you speak to me, you vile little sneak?"

"You're a bully!" said Claude, the hot anger flushing his face.

Worden sprang forward, and with his open palm struck him a blow over the eye that sent the boy to the floor.

He arose with the stinging pains in his leg redoubled in their intensity.

"Now, will you be civil, and do as you're told?" continued Worden, his face very grim and an ugly light in his eyes.

"No," said Claude; and he meant it.

Such a cruel face as the little lad gazed upon! Cruelty is a mystery, and its father is a mystery. There is a certain class of sins that gradually blinds the mind, enfeebles the will and forces out of even the youthful heart every spark of kindness and of love. There is a certain class of sins which strikes like a frost upon the heart, blights every bud of promise, and puts forth in place thereof the weeds of selfishness and cruelty.

Claude saw the *effects* of such sins, he knew nothing of the *cause*. He had never before seen to what awful depths cruelty could go. To him these faces were as much a mystery as is life to the student of science. Now he stood face to face with sin in its hideous consequences; he the pure, the innocent, the devout, with the cleansing waters of sacramental absolution still fresh upon his spirit. Here you have a picture with two sides, my young reader: sin on one, sinlessness on the other. Yours it must be to choose. Claude did not perceive the force of this picture, for he did not understand all that lay behind the cruelty of those faces. But later on, as this narrative unfolds, he saw the same picture again in clearer light, in other circumstances, and he understood it.

Worden took the buggy whip from behind the door. "Now, sir, if you don't obey, I'll horsewhip you till the blood comes!"

"What do you want me to do?" asked Claude.

"Begin by turning a handspring."

"Very well; let me start from the door there."

And Claude stepped over till he was near the door against which Worden was leaning.

Looking straight ahead of him as though

measuring the distance, he took two steps forward, then raised his arms in the air as if about to spring. Suddenly both arms flew out, one to his right, one to his left, and while one hand snatched the lighted cigar from the long-legged young man's mouth, the other seized the coal-oil can; and before a single one of the lookers-on could realize what had come to pass, Claude was standing beside the hay, the cigar in one hand held just directly over the hay where the inverted can was soaking it with coal oil. And in the same instant—for it all came about in a flash—he shouted out:

"If one of you moves a step, I'll drop this cigar!"

Chapter XI

IN WHICH CLAUDE MAKES HIS ESCAPE

THERE was courage in Claude's flashing eyes, determination in his set face, though the mouth was partially open to relieve his heavy breathing. He looked neither at cigar nor at oil can but kept his eyes fixed steadily upon the three, who had turned ashen pale.

Not one of them moved; not one of them uttered a word; it was as though all had been gorgonized.

"What do you wish?" Worden finally gasped; for the steady eye of Claude had cowed him, and he feared in the ignorance of his heart that any imprudence on his part would be the signal for an explosion followed by the burning of his father's stable. None of these three ruffians was at all familiar with chemistry.

"I give you fellows one minute to go down there on the lawn and stand where I can see you from that window."

"Come on, fellows, or I'll never hear the end of this," said Worden, still in a whisper.

Claude moved not till they were out of the room. Then as the last one disappeared, he arose, put the cigar in his mouth and puffed at it vigorously. He was not done with it yet, and it would not serve his purpose were the light to go out. Claude, like Worden, was of opinion that a lighted cigar dropped upon coal oil would produce an instantaneous blaze.

He walked over to the window, this small boy, still puffing away at the cigar. A passer-by looking up would have laughed; the innocent young face and the burning cigar looked so incongruous. But the three rowdies as they came upon the lawn and stared up at the window did not laugh, for they now knew that it was possible to hold a small boy in respect.

Claude, as he blew out clouds of smoke, took in the situation. The stable faced upon an alley near Thirteenth Street, and running up to Fourteenth.

"I'll keep this cigar lighted," said Claude as he removed it from his mouth, "till you fellows go up that alley as far as Fourteenth Street. And you'd better hurry, too, for I'm in dead earnest. And don't dare turn your heads on the way."

As though they had been his slaves, the three hurried out of the yard, into the alley, and ran in the direction indicated as though their lives depended upon it. As they went through the gate, Claude clattered down the stairway and, gaining the alley, set off at the top of his speed for Thirteenth Street. He did not succeed as well as he had hoped; for before he had reached the street, his enemies, who had gained the corner of Fourteenth, turned just in time to see him. With a loud cry they started in pursuit.

Poor Claude! His race had cost him dear. His right leg refused to stand further strain, and he could hear the sharp footfalls of his pursuers as they clattered up the alley. Further running was out of the question. He looked about him. At his side was a lawn, back of which rose a handsome residence. Without a moment's hesitation Claude hobbled in by the open gateway, made the porch with difficulty and, crawling under it, lay quiet till he heard his pursuers turn the corner in full cry and dash up the street.

He had no small trouble in emerging from his hiding place, and with much pain and labor, picking his way by every odd and end that could yield him support, he walked, or rather crawled to the kitchen, and knocked.

"Come in," said a voice.

The door opened, and the cook raised her hands in horror as she saw a small boy, his clothes covered with dirt, his face bleeding and very pale, standing hatless and in an attitude of entreaty at the door.

Then she gave a cry as the little figure toppled over, face foremost, and lay still and senseless upon the floor.

Claude had fainted from pain.

Chapter XII

IN WHICH KATE AND CLAUDE ARE
BITTERLY DISAPPOINTED

"ARE you better, my poor boy?" Claude as he opened his eyes and caught these words saw that he was in a luxuriously furnished room and that a refined lady was bending over him, while she applied smelling salts to his nostrils.

"I can't move it," said Claude with a groan.

"What, dear?"

"My leg, ma'am. Oh, please have me taken home; I'm afraid I shall not be able to go out tomorrow. Oh, dear—it's hard."

"Indeed, my little boy, you must stay quiet for some days."

Claude groaned again. Ah! He had set his heart upon that First Communion morning.

"What is your name?"

"Claude Lightfoot, ma'am."

"And how did you come to be so hurt?"

"I can't tell the story now, ma'am. Some boys handled me roughly; I had hurt my leg some days ago, and now it's worse; and tomorrow was to be my First Communion day."

A doctor, who had been summoned when Claude swooned, now entered. He examined the little patient and said easily:

"Oh, it's of no consequence; the boy will be about as well as ever in a week."

And he was very much astonished when Claude stifled a sob and turned his face away.

"What's the matter, boy? Are you afraid to lie in bed?"

"It's an ugly dream," said Claude. "Oh, please take me home."

"Can he be moved safely, doctor?" asked the lady.

"Yes, but he must be carried with great care."

"And I'm your man to see to that," said a brisk, good-humored young man of nineteen or twenty, who had just entered. "The coachman is waiting outside, and if you, little fellow, will trust me, I'll carry you as though you were made of glass."

Claude held out his hand to the lady.

"Thank you, ma'am, very much. If you please, I'll come to see you when I get well, and thank you again and tell you all about it. But just now I feel too bad. Good-bye."

"God bless you!" said the lady very gently. She was a mother, and knew how sacred were the sorrows of children.

"Was it that brute of a Worden that got

you into this fix?" asked young Mr. Andrews as the carriage rumbled over the street.

"How did you guess?" cried Claude in astonishment.

"If anything goes wrong about here, it's six to one that he's in it. Cheer up, little boy. You mustn't take your trouble too hard."

"But you don't understand all," said Claude.

And then, won by Mr. Andrews' sympathy, and revived by the light evening breeze, he told his story. Mr. Andrews listened in amazement; for despite Claude's modesty and unassumingness in the telling, his listener succeeded in piecing out the boy's bravery and determination throughout the sad ordeal.

"Little boy, you're a trump," he said warmly, "and you're worth a dozen by yourself. If I weren't a civilized man and in a civilized city, I'd give that Worden *such* a cowhiding." And Mr. Andrews clinched his fists.

"Please don't touch him, sir, on my account. I guess I'm done with him. It was partly my own fault anyhow. And now, sir, I'm beginning to feel bad about the way I acted in that loft. I lost my temper awfully, and it was just after Confession."

Our little friend was beginning to suffer scruples. As I have already said, he was quick to act, and afterward prone to find wrongdoing where he had acted either without reflection, or where he had followed, as he saw matters, what at the time appeared to be reasonable.

"Well, sir!" exclaimed Mr. Andrews, with strong emphasis on the 'sir,' "if ever you do nothing worse than that you'll go straight to Heaven."

He added a moment later:

"Claude, I'm not of your religion; in fact, I'm not much on any sort of religion, but when you do go to Communion, won't you say a little prayer for me?"

"I'll be very glad, Mr. Andrews."

"And, my boy, if ever you want a friend and don't know where to go, just call on me. I can't say how glad I am to have met you; and mother will be very much disappointed, and so shall I, if you don't pay us that visit as you promised her."

"You're very kind, sir," said Claude, brightening.

"Ah, here we are," continued Mr. Andrews, as the carriage drew up at the sidewalk facing Mr. Lightfoot's house and the driver threw open the door. "If you can manage to walk, Claude, by leaning on me, it will look better and not scare your people so much."

"I'll try, sir."

But the effort was beyond Claude, and while the coachman preceded them and rang the bell, Mr. Andrews carried his charge in his arms.

"Don't be alarmed," said the young man as the servant threw open the door. "Claude has injured his leg again."

There was a rustle and a quick movement, and Kate came hurrying down the stairs, very pale, but under great restraint.

"My dear," she said, ignoring the stranger's presence and, after kissing Claude, fixing her eyes intently upon his face, "what has happened?"

"It's nothing, Kate; only I can't walk."

Kate's features worked, and her bosom heaved with emotion; but with a mighty effort she restrained her feelings.

"Mama must not know it too suddenly, dear. Sir, would you kindly carry him to his bedroom after me—and very softly, sir, for my mother is an invalid and we must not shock her."

And Kate led the way, praying for strength.

"Kate," said Claude when he lay resting upon the white-covered bed which no hand but his sister's ever arranged, "I want you to know this gentleman, who has been ever so kind to me, Mr. Andrews."

"Thank you, thank you a thousand times, Mr. Andrews, for your goodness toward my brother."

"Don't mention it, Kate. I am glad to meet the sister of such a brother. And now," added Mr. Andrews with a fine delicacy, "I'll take my leave, as I have an important engagement, and beg permission to call on you with my mother tomorrow."

And Mr. Andrews left, a better, wiser man for what little he had seen of Kate and Claude.

Then Kate, having conducted Mr. Andrews to the door, returned, laid her cheek beside that of her brother and put her arm round his neck. But she said nothing.

"What's the matter, Kit? Why don't you talk?"

There was no answer.

"Say, Kit, it's hard, awful; it's just too bad: I can't go to Holy Communion tomorrow."

The arm tightened about his neck, but still no answer.

"I feel as bad about it as I can feel about anything, Kit. It seems to pull at my heart. Say, Kit, why don't you ask me to tell how it all happened?"

Then he heard a sob and raised his head

with a start.

"Why, Kit, you're *crying; that's* what's the matter. Oh, please don't. I can't bear it to see you give up. Kit, I'm a fool, I'm a wretched—I don't know what. I might have known that it would come harder on you than on me, and here I go on talking as if I was the only one in it. Now, Kit, I can stand it—you see if I can't. I'll never complain again. Stop crying, Kit, and I'll laugh and show you I can stand a knock as well as anyone."

And there Claude paused in unspeakable distress, for Kate sighed and sobbed as though her heart were breaking. Claude's joys and sorrows were hers, and the girl, even had Claude not spoken, could picture vividly her brother's sorrow and distress.

"Kit," continued Claude, "it's only the difference of a few days; and I'll be prepared all the better. I will. Then it will be just the same as if nothing had happened. The pain is all over now, Kit, and you'll see that I won't bother one bit."

Claude spoke the truth. In his distress at seeing his sister's burst of grief and in his self-reproach at awakening her sorrow, he had, as far as the will goes, fully resigned himself to the inevitable delay.

At length Kate raised her face and looked down upon him.

"I couldn't help it, dear," she said softly; "it was cruel of me—"

"No, it wasn't," roared Claude.

"But I had to have my cry out. And now that's over, Claude, and we'll begin again. We had set our hearts on our First Communion, Claude, and we weren't ready for such a shock, were we?"

"That's so," answered Claude.

"But now we're going to go on, just the same as if nothing had gone wrong."

"Yes, Kit; we're both able to stand it now." And Claude told his story, but in such a way that instead of figuring as the hero he made himself out to be the villain. He made light of Worden's cruelty, made light of the pain he had suffered, and dilated upon his own burst of anger. But Kate knew her brother, knew that his tender conscience exaggerated the evil of what he had done, and she at once cheered him and relieved his scruples in a few happy words.

Then, wiping her eyes, she left Claude to break the news to her mother.

She performed her task well. She led Mrs. Lightfoot so gently to understanding the case that the shock and disappointment were reduced to a minimum.

The father, when he returned, heard the news with dismay. He was strangely vexed; he saw that Claude was in nowise to blame, but his disappointment had to vent itself on something or someone, and he chose Claude. The little boy on his bed of pain listened humbly to his father's scolding.

"I deserved it, Kit," he said that night. "Pa knows that if I had behaved at school, Worden would have left me alone. But I'll be out in a few days, and we'll make it all right next Sunday.

Claude was again reckoning without his host.

Chapter XIII

IN WHICH MR. RUSSEL UNWITTINGLY PROPHESIES

MR. LIGHTFOOT, on the following day, grew somewhat reconciled to his disappointment. He spoke very kindly to Claude and did all in his power to console him.

But when a question arose of choosing

some other Sunday for Claude's First Communion, the father's prejudices came into play. Mr. Lightfoot considered the blazing of many candles, the pomp of priestly vestments, the organ peal and a number of boys in white kid gloves and of girls with blue sashes and crowns of flowers as being almost essential to the proper making of First Communion. He could no more conceive of one boy's making his First Communion alone than he could conceive of one bird's flocking together by itself. There could be no pomp, no dignity, no display where one boy was concerned. To omit this pomp, this dignity, this display on so striking an occasion would be un-American. In the end it came to this, that Claude was to make his First Communion when and where the ceremonies came sufficiently up to Mr. Lightfoot's standards of Americanism. This threw very little light upon the subject, Mr. Lightfoot's standard on this point being known to no one, including himself.

Claude was kept quite busy for four days entertaining many visitors and receiving their condolences. All who called were astonished at his cheerfulness and mirth; many judged that the mischance had caused him no sorrow. Claude and Kate said nothing of Worden to the college boy visitors, for they feared that should Elmwood or Collins or Winter learn of his cruelty, the bully might have to render a hard account.

On Friday, Claude started for school with as happy a face as though he had never known a trial. It was a beautiful morning, and the sound of a few singing birds that had strayed into the Avenue fell delightfully upon his ears, while the clear, cool air, the odor of flowers, and the fresh, green lawns—were there ever such lawns, so green, so trim, as those that adorn the Avenue of Milwaukee?—all these things, I say, filled him with happiness. What a pleasure it was to feel his feet firm beneath him, to leap, to bound in healthful youth and happy innocence. Claude felt what a great joy it was to be well again, and he was happy as a lark. To leave nothing wanting, he came upon a tin can and had the exquisite pleasure of kicking it full two squares.

"Hello, little man!" exclaimed Mr. Russel as the cheerful youth tripped in at the college gate.

"How de do, sir?" responded Claude as he doffed his cap and burst into a radiancy of smile.

"I'm glad to see you. Come on here, and sit down; I want to have a talk with you."

Mr. Russel, who was stationed in the yard each morning, partly to greet the boys, partly to urge the loiterers in to studies, led Claude over to the bench.

"Claude," he began, "I'm glad your Communion was put off."

Claude looked surprised.

"So you don't believe me?"

"Yes, sir, if you say so."

"I do say it. Look here, Claude, I've been thinking about your case a good deal, and the more I think, the surer I feel that it was a good thing that it turned out the way it did."

"You didn't think I was good enough, sir."

"I didn't say any such thing. No: the more I thought of it, the more I felt convinced that you were the best prepared boy in the class. And that's the reason I felt glad that you were put off."

Claude broke into a giggle.

"You needn't make fun of me," said the prefect in his most serious way.

"I'm not, sir; but it seems so funny to hear that I was put off because I was so well-prepared."

"It seems funny, but it isn't. And the reason why I stick to my opinion is because I know that God's ways are not our ways. Do you understand?"

"No, sir."

"Who said you did? Well, here's the case. You knew your catechism like a book. You made every effort to get over your faults. You prayed hard, and you learned your lessons, and you stopped fidgeting in class as near as it is possible for you to do so, and when you lost your temper and talked back to Mr. Grace, you did penance for it in sackcloth and ashes—"

"I think not, sir."

"Little boy, I speak in figures. And Father Maynard considered you the best prepared boy of all, and so did the president and the vice president, and your teacher was anxious for you to make your First Communion—"

"Was he, sir?"

"Of course he was; and so was I. And I prayed for you every day, and he prayed for you."

"You did?" exclaimed Claude in astonishment.

"Can't you believe anything I say? Of course we did. We don't measure the importance of people by their size. Well now, let me go on. There was that sister of yours. She's as good a girl as any I know of. She was praying and working with you—"

"Yes, indeed, sir: she did more than I did."

"And your Mama was praying to see the day, and in fact, we were all anxious for it. And then you made a great Confession, a splendid Confession."

"How did you know that, sir?"

"Didn't I see you coming out of the chapel with a smile that was worth getting patented, it was so happy? Now look you, Claude; everything was in your favor, and still you were held back. Who held you back?"

"God," said Claude.

"Boy, you've got brains. It *was* God; it was by His permission that you were held back. Now, Claude, I'm only thirty years old, but I've tried to keep my eyes open all my life; and if a man does that, he can see as much in thirty years as another can in sixty; and I tell you, Claude, that, as far as I can judge from all that I've known and seen and read, I tell you that God has allowed you to be put off because He has special designs on you. He has taken the matter out of our little hands into His own. Keep up your courage, my little man, and each day as you arise try to act as though that day were to be your Communion day. It's coming—you don't know when, I don't know when. But come it will, when and where God pleases. He will dispose of all things sweetly, and it is my honest belief that when God does come to you, my little man, He will come with special and wondrous graces. There, Claude, that's my opinion."

Mr. Russel in these latter words had dropped his tone of banter; his face had taken on a look of earnestness; and his heart kindled his words into what sounded like inspiration. One could see that he meant what he said, that he was speaking from strong conviction. And yet had he learned at that moment how close he had come upon the actual facts, how literally his words forecast what was to come, he would have been astounded.

This high, lovely and consoling spirituality fell upon willing ears and penetrated a noble heart.

"Mr. Russel," said Claude, arising and taking the prefect's hand, "I can't say what I'd like to say. People don't know how I've been feeling, for I've kept it to myself, but now it's all gone, and I'm happier than ever. And I won't forget what you've said—not one word."

And as Claude went into the chapel, he said to himself:

"Oh, if I could only grow up to be a man like him!"

And Mr. Russel thought:

"That little mite will be able to teach me anything, whether in virtue or learning, before I'm fifty."

Chapter XIV

CLAUDE was not the only boy whose First Communion was put off. On the second day of the retreat, Willie Hardy was told by Father Maynard to wait another year. Willie was a remarkably pretty boy, with an innocent face and a constant smile. He was quiet and had a habit of taking his hat off whether to father, prefect or professor, with the prettiest air imaginable. He had entered college three days after Claude and thus far was a favorite with the faculty and the most unpopular youngster in the yard. Willie was in a way a diplomat. He showed his velvet to his teachers, his claws to the boys. When the news spread that he was not to make his

First Communion, there was a great surprise: but among his mates, little regret. I said just now that he was disliked; it would have been more proper to say that he was held in contempt. Willie Hardy was an habitual liar.

He noticed Claude closely on the day of our lively friend's return to college, and it struck his fancy that perhaps Claude, who now tripped about as though his limbs had never known injury, had pretended lameness and thus saved himself from the imputation of being considered unfit to approach the Blessed Sacrament. To Willie this seemed very probable; he considered Claude a bad boy. Had Claude not laughed at his lisp? Had Claude not poked him in the ribs and crushed his stiff hat? All these things in Willie's eyes were very wicked. Now the step from "it may be so" in Willie's mind to "it is so" had been worn down so effectually by constant lying that they were almost flush with each other.

"I thay, Frank," he cried, running up flushed and eager and pretty to Elmwood, who was talking with Collins, "did you hear the newth?"

"What's the matter now?" asked Frank.

"Lightfoot thickneth wath all in hith eye."

"Thickness! Thickness!" echoed Frank. "What the mischief does anybody care about Lightfoot's thickness?"

"I didn't say thickneth," cried Willie with a captivating smile, "I said—" here he took breath and, with an effort, said—"thickneth."

I really think that Willie's lisp had been a help to him in his career of lying. It was a charming lisp, and grown folks had been so much taken up with the prettiness of his pronunciation as to pay little or no attention to what he said. Thus many of his Arabian statements had been allowed to pass unchecked, while people fell into ecstasies over his lisp.

"Perhaps you mean sickness, Sissie," said Frank, unsoftened by the blandishments of the pretty boy.

"Yeth; Lightfoot played off; he wathn't to make hith Firth Communion anyhow. Father Maynard told me tho himthelf. He thaid that he'd rather let me go than Claude, becauthe Claude wath the wortht boy in the yard." At the end of this clear and accurate statement of fact, Willie folded his hands and looked positively celestial. Frank and Rob, on the other hand, looked "of the earth, earthly"— Frank's face, in particular, becoming very grim.

"Are you lying, as usual?"

"Croth my heart," protested Willie, "ith the truth, and nothing elthe."

Frank gave a growl and, catching his angelic informant by the collar, proceeded very rapidly toward the college building.

"Wath the matter, Frank?" asked Willie, making no attempt to struggle.

"I'm going to Father Maynard's room with you to find out from his own lips if what you've said is true."

"Father Maynard ithn't in. I thaw him jumping on a threet car going downtown jutht two minuth ago."

"Heavings!" exclaimed Collins, who had kept abreast of Frank. "There's Father Maynard standing at his window now and reading his breviary. Sissie, if all your lies were glued together, they'd make a walking track from here to San Francisco."

"I've a notion to put your head in the tub," added Frank.

"No, no: pleathe don't do that. You'll thpoil my new collar. I take it back, Frank. It wath all a joke."

Giving the sweet youth, who, by the way, was highly perfumed, a squeeze that elicited a shriek, Frank released his hold, saying as he did so:

"You'd better not tell that lie to anyone else."

"Oh, no, Frank; I wath jutht going to tell you how it wath a joke when you rumpled my collar. I'll not thay another word about it."

And then Willie with his sweet smile hurried away and, before the end of recess, had told the same story to nineteen or twenty boys of his own age. It is no slight tribute to his reputation to add that not a single boy believed him. Several were good enough to tell him plainly and unequivocally that he was lying, whereupon Willie without change of color or show of surprise would cross his heart and go on protesting the truth of every word.

It was seldom that his fancy hit upon so damaging a lie, and he did not take into account that a lie aimed at a person's reputation is far more serious in its character than one that is harmful chiefly to the teller. He learned this distinction that afternoon when the vice president read him a homily before the class, then took the youngster to his room and returned him five minutes later all in tears and sobs and blushes.

Claude was the last to hear the story, and he laughed till the tears ran down his cheeks. After Willie's whipping, he was the first and only boy to condole with the talented liar.

"It wath a joke," protested Willie between his sobs. Then he borrowed ten cents of Claude and owes him that money to this day.

The months of May and June passed quickly. Claude kept Mr. Russel's prediction in mind, and he rose each day with the determination to be as good as possible. But it was one thing to resolve, and another to carry out the resolution. He was still giddy, restless and impulsive. Mr. Grace was very gentle with him, for he really and thoroughly sympathized with the little boy in his trial; but for all that, he thought it his duty to call Claude to task quite frequently; and Claude, it must be said, took his punishment with an equal mind.

In the yard, Claude often ran foul of the more dignified young students, and, on the whole, his record was not satisfactory.

"I do my thinking after it's all over," he used to say; and then he would go off to Confession and relieve himself of his scruples.

Even Mr. Russel was sometimes discouraged.

"See here, Claude," he said one day when his impulsive friend had been within a little of being crushed under the heels of the larger boys in a football rush; "if you don't get some prudence into your head, you'll never grow up to cultivate a mustache. Didn't I tell you that small boys are not allowed to play football with the big boys?"

"I didn't think, sir."

"Well, it's about time for you to take thought. Get your history, my little man."

Claude learned his twenty-five lines and, that very afternoon, on his way downtown to meet his sister, escaped almost by a miracle from under the hoofs of a team of horses.

Claude himself was inclined to despair; but Kate, gentle and firm, never gave up. She waited and prayed for the day when her brother would awake to a sense of thoughtfulness and prudence.

At the closing exhibition our little friend won the silver medal in elocution, and first premiums in history, geography, Christian doctrine, reading and spelling. In Latin, in English grammar and in composition—branches which require application—he received no mention. It is superfluous to add that his name was not recorded on the list of students distinguished for excellent deportment.

Thus after three months at a Catholic school, we find Claude still setting the same problem to Frank Elmwood. Trials and resolutions had had full play, and yet no material change had taken place.

On the morning after the distribution of prizes, Frank Elmwood called at Claude's house.

"I want to see your father!" said Frank very shortly, and in much excitement.

Claude called his father and, with a certain instinctive delicacy, left the two alone in the parlor.

"Sir," said Frank, after the customary interchange of greeting, "I came to ask you a great favor."

"Well?"

"Winter and I and Dan Dockery and Willie Hardy and Charles Pierson are going to camp out for a few weeks at Lake Vesper, about thirty miles from here. A number of the college boys are to board at houses near us, and, as you know, the Collins people have a villa there and are within a few minutes' walk of the place where we're going to pitch our tent. Now, sir, we have plenty of room for one more: Dockery and Pierson are special friends of Claude's, and it would be splendid if you'd let Claude come along. All the fellows want it."

"It's an outing, what they call an outing,"

said Mr. Lightfoot, stroking his chin reflectively. "I rather like the idea myself. Outing is such a thoroughly American way of doing things."

"We've got over ten dollars' worth of fireworks for the Fourth of July, sir; and we're going to have a jolly bonfire. And on the morning of the Fourth we're going to have six American flags stuck about our tent."

"Excellent!" exclaimed Mr. Lightfoot, clapping his hand upon Frank's back. "But you shall have a dozen flags and another ten dollars' worth of fireworks—I shall send them myself."

"But what about Claude—may he come?"

"I'm decidedly in favor of it. I'm highly pleased with what you've told me. But on a question like that I must consult my wife, and, of course, Kate. Just wait one moment. Claude," he called, going to the door.

"Yes, Papa."

"Ask your mama and sister to step this way for a moment."

Mrs. Lightfoot, whose ancestors had fought and bled for the cause of independence, betrayed a curious want of interest concerning the number of American flags, but was very searching in her questions as to what measures had been taken for cooking, sleeping accommodations and shelter. Frank gave sufficiently satisfactory replies, and after a conference of some three-quarters of an hour, Mrs. Lightfoot and Kate gracefully yielded their assent. Then Claude was summoned.

How his eyes danced when he heard what had been decided upon! He ran up to Frank and pounded him affectionately on the back, and Frank smiled while smothering the pain; for Claude's strokes were as strong as they were affectionate.

"Now, my dear," said the mother, "I put you in full charge of Frank as long as you're away; and you are to obey him as you would me."

"Yes, Mama, I'll do it."

"And," added Frank, "I'll be as careful of Claude as I know how."

"How are you off for hammocks?" asked Mr. Lightfoot.

"Well, the truth is, sir, I've been put to so much expense buying necessaries that I've put off getting such extras till next year."

"Since Claude is going," continued Mr. Lightfoot, "it's my duty to take a share in the expenses."

"We didn't count on that, sir."

"Oh, I'll do the counting. Now if you've

time, you might go down to Carroll & Kennedy's notion store and get, say, three hammocks. If they haven't any in stock, they'll very willingly order them for you."

"Thank you ever so much, sir. The boys will be delighted."

"It's the American way of doing things in the country," said Mr. Lightfoot. "And, by the way, when you and Claude go downtown, you might find something or other that hasn't occurred to me. Now, for instance, have you balls and bats?"

"We have an old ball and a couple of bats, sir."

"Oh, you must do better than that by baseball; it's the national game. Here are ten dollars, and you can buy whatever suits you in that line."

"I'm almost ashamed to take it, sir."

"You needn't hold back, Elmwood. It's a kindness in you to take such interest in my little boy; and it's only just that I should help along. Of course, you must keep account of expenses for provisions and the like, and I'll pay my quota for that too."

Claude, who had been dancing in and out among the chairs, now sprang forward eagerly.

"Come on, Frank: it's near ten o'clock;

let's hurry down after those baseballs and hammocks."

"If I'm not mistaken, Carroll & Kennedy keep open till seven in the evening," said Papa; "so if you both hurry, you may still get there before the store closes."

Too intent upon his own plans to perceive this paternal joke, Claude almost pulled his friend out of the room. He was seen a moment later clearing the fence at a bound and heard yelling at the top of his voice.

Chapter XV

IN WHICH CLAUDE AMUSES HIMSELF WITH A BULL

MRS. LIGHTFOOT, in the interview touched upon in the last chapter, had been anxious to learn into what kind of company her little boy would be thrown.

"Oh," Frank had said, "they're a good set. Winter is a little gentleman, and he's a weekly communicant. He's a good fellow, even if he is a little frisky now and then; but most boys that I know are that way, too.

Dockery and Pierson are full of fun and life—
especially Dockery; but they are both as good
as any small boys I know of. Then there's
Willie Hardy—um—"

Frank smiled and blushed.

"What about Willie?" asked Mrs. Lightfoot.

"I didn't want him along, but his mother
begged me to take him. She's a widow and,
I believe, a very pious woman. She just dotes
on Willie, who's her only child. I guess she
has spoiled him. He's too young to be bad,
but he is an infernal—that is, he gets a freak
occasionally and won't tell the truth under
any circumstances."

"Lying is un-American," observed Mr. Lightfoot. He never said anything truer. Lying is
un-American. The writer of this story, when
he thinks of the true American boy, always
thinks of one whose foremost trait is downright honesty. During the whole of this conference, it may be remarked, Mr. Lightfoot's
hobby appeared at its best. "Outing" is American, and so, too, is baseball.

"Has Willie Hardy much influence over his
companions?" pursued Mrs. Lightfoot.

"Influence!" cried Frank. "They hardly show
him the common signs of respect. Willie has
been trying hard to tell the truth this month.
I threatened not to take him if he didn't stop

lying. Now he generally stops to think before he answers. Whenever he does this, I know he's telling the truth. But whenever he answers without hesitation, I begin to doubt. You see, the boy labors in telling the truth and lies without effort."

Convinced that Willie could have no evil influence over Claude, Mrs. Lightfoot turned to other points and ended, as we saw in the last chapter, by deciding that her son might join the camping party.

The "outing" began most favorably. Frank Elmwood had seen to every detail, and to their simple comfort nothing was wanting. Much of the work fell upon John Winter and Frank, the smaller members of the party devoting themselves almost exclusively for the first three days to swimming and to rambles in the woods.

Claude returned each day with his knee breeches in a condition that called for repairing, and the service of a neighbor had to be invoked to keep this indefatigable climber of trees in patches. Luckily he had brought four pairs of knickerbockers, and Frank was thinking seriously of sending for four more.

Their camp stood a little back of an arm of Lake Vesper, or rather of a separate lake, for it was connected with the larger body of water by a narrow channel. Some few minutes' walk to the west of them was situated the villa belonging to Mr. Collins, which commanded a view of the greater water. Beyond Mr. Collins' lawn lay a great open field which answered every requirement for baseball purposes, and, as its margin gave an excellent place for bathing, this field was a favorite rendezvous of the boys.

It was here that Claude took his lesson in swimming. I say lesson, for one was enough. Under Frank's direction, he caught the trick of balancing himself in the water, and he required no further assistance. Far from Claude's needing encouragement, Frank was obliged to keep a close eye on him, as the youngster persisted in going out of his depth and paddled about as though the waters were his natural home. In the water as on shore, Claude had a certain instinct for anything that called for play and flexibility of muscle, and his quickness in learning astonished all.

How Frank contrived to attend to the camp and keep track of Claude is a mystery. But he was unfailing in his vigilance.

His only resting time came when Claude was engaged at baseball or in bed. Then he knew that the young scapegrace was safe.

One morning after their usual swim, John and Frank, taking it for granted that the little boys would, as usual, play "knock-up" till dinner time, departed for the camp to prepare dinner. Archer, who was staying at a farmhouse, Walter Collins, Dockery, Pierson and Claude took the field, while Rob Collins batted them high flies. An unlucky hit of Rob's sent the ball into a bit of marshy land near the lake, and despite their search, they could discover no trace of it. Just as they were abandoning the quest, Rob's mother sent word that he was needed at the house, and thus it came about that the six small boys were left to their own resources.

"Did any of you see the bull up in Livingstone's pasture?" asked Archer.

"Is he a big fellow?" cried Claude.

"He's a beauty; come on, he's worth seeing."

"I've got a red handkerchief," said Claude, "and maybe we'll have a little fun."

"You'd better look out," said Walter Collins, who was a quiet, calm, prudent little fellow. He never ran blindly into danger, but in it, he was as courageous as Claude.

"Come along, Collins!" cried Archer, as the crowd started off at a trot up the slope leading inland.

"No, I'll not."

Now if there was one of these small boys who understood Claude, it was young Collins; and understanding him as he did, he feared that Claude would put himself in danger in order to have "fun" with the bull. So, after a moment's thought, he set off at a smart run for the camp.

"I say, Frank!" he shouted breathlessly, as he came within cry, "the fellows have all gone up to take a look at Livingstone's bull, and Claude's got a red handkerchief and says he's going to have some fun."

Dashing a partially peeled potato to the ground, Frank arose, and without waiting to pull off a sort of apron that protected his trousers, he set off bareheaded and at full speed in the direction of Livingstone's field, followed at an ever-increasing distance by Walter Collins. At length, arriving breathless at the top of a hill which commanded a good view, Frank saw a sight which filled him with dismay.

Nearly a quarter of a mile to the west lay a pasture land of twelve or thirteen acres, inclosed by a stout, strong fence, some five feet six inches high. At the end of the field nearest him, and just outside the fence, stood a group of boys, apparently in a state of uncontrollable delight. Inside

the fence stood Claude, hopping and dancing, as he flaunted a gay red rag in the
breeze; and rushing down from the further
end of the pasture came Livingstone's bull.
Frank stood fixed in horror. Nearer and
nearer drew the furious beast, lashing his
tail and pawing up the ground, while the
young scapegrace danced and hopped as
though the animal bearing down upon him
were a spring lamb.

"Oh, Collins, what shall I do?" shouted
Frank, still staring at the spectacle.

The bull came straight on, and was within
five yards of Claude when the lad suddenly
vaulted over the fence and forthwith doubled up, apparently with laughter, at the
wide-eyed stupid discomfiture of his pursuer.

"Thank God! He's safe," exclaimed Frank
heartily. "But if the little rat had missed his
hold in vaulting, he might have been gored
to death. Hallo! What are they up to now?"

For the boys, led by Claude, were hurrying toward the other end of the field in such
a manner as not to attract the attention of
his enraged majesty.

"Why, Frank!" cried Walter, "I do believe
he's going to try it over again."

With an impatient exclamation, Frank
broke into a run, determined, if possible, to

put an end to this foolhardy bull-baiting. But before he had left the hill behind him, the merrymaker below had again jumped into the arena.

"Hi! Hi!" he shouted, waving the rag and dancing in glee. "Hi! Hi! Come on here with your old bull head."

The beast turned angrily and, awaiting no further invitation, gave a bellow and came raging down the field.

Frank found himself racing against the bull, and with very slender prospects of success. As the bull got quite near, and Frank came within hailing distance, he could contain himself no longer.

"Claude! Claude!" he cried in agony. This step was unfortunate; Claude heard his name called when the furious beast was nearly upon him and looked in the direction whence the call proceeded.

"Look out, Claude! Look out!" came a chorus of frightened voices from his companions.

Claude turned to see the bull within a few feet of him. Quick as a flash, he put his hand upon the top railing of the fence; but before he could clear it, the head of the bull was beneath his feet, and Claude went high, high into the air propelled by that strong head and came down flat on his face, but, most fortunately, on the safe side of the fence.

He rose to greet the palest faces he had ever seen. But he dispelled their fear by breaking into a shout of laughter.

"Oh, didn't I fool him!" he exclaimed. "It was rich!"

"Young man," said Frank, hardly able to control himself, "do you know that you were within an inch of losing your life?"

"An inch is as good as a mile," retorted Claude lightly. And then he became very much astonished when he saw how grave Frank had become.

"If there were an asylum for fools," bawled Frank indignantly to the whole party, "I'd have you all admitted at once!"

"We didn't want Claude to go into that field," said Dockery. "But Willie Hardy stumped him to do it, and then we couldn't keep him back—could we, Archer?"

"Sure," answered Archer.

"And then when he did get in and began dancing around, we were pretty nervous the first time, but after that—"

"For goodness sake!" broke in Frank, "how many times did he jump into that field?"

"The last was the fourth time," answered Archer. "He hopped over the fence so lightly and easily the first time the bull came to him that we thought there wouldn't be any danger. But each time he tried it, he let the bull get nearer, and you saw what happened last time."

"He tore my pants!" said Claude ruefully; "it's my fourth pair."

"Confound your pants!" said Frank. "Claude, as long as you're out here, don't you go near that bull again."

"I won't Frank; I wouldn't have gone in for all the stumps in the world if I had thought you wouldn't like it."

"Well, I'm blessed!" exclaimed Frank. "So you thought I'd have enjoyed it if I'd been here, I suppose."

"Well, it was great fun," answered Claude. Which shows how little sense of personal danger Claude had. It was such occurrences as this that gave his older friends so much anxiety. The boy was honest, and willing to do what was proper, but his appreciation of danger was so little that he could scarcely be trusted out of sight.

"Willie Hardy," continued Frank, "if you do any more stumping in regard to Claude, I'll send you home."

"I didn't think he wath thutch a fool," said the pretty boy. Frank rewarded this answer with a withering glance. But Willie, quite satisfied with his explanation, was already preparing to astound the folks at home with a thrilling account of a bullfight in which he himself was to figure as the hero.

As the party, somewhat crestfallen, made for the camp, gentle Willie ran on ahead and startled the ladies at the Collins' villa with the announcement that Claude had been nearly gored to death by a bull.

The boy had a passion for lying.

Claude walked, for good reasons, in the rear of the procession, and, after a process of hard thinking, still failed to see why Frank Elmwood was so angry.

Chapter XVI

IN WHICH CLAUDE TAKES TO POETRY

ABOUT ten days after their arrival at their camping grounds on Lake Vesper, John Winter remarked to Frank:

"Haven't you noticed that Pierson and Dockery avoid one another of late?"

"Now that you speak of it," said Frank,

"it strikes me that there is some sort of coolness between them."

"And another thing, Archer doesn't come near our fellows anymore."

"What do you think is the matter, John?"

"I can't say: it's worth looking into."

"Claude," called Frank, looking up toward the sky.

"Well!" exclaimed Claude, from the outer end of a branch twenty-five feet above their heads.

"Say, you'll break your neck if that branch gives way. Come down: I want to talk with you."

"I'm not going to break my neck, Frank; I'm learning a new way of getting off a tree."

Before Frank could interpose, Claude, catching hold of the very tip of the branch, swung himself off. The branch bent beneath his weight and brought him several feet nearer ground. Then Claude, swinging in the air, cast his eyes about. He quickly found what he wanted, for with a slight spring he let go his hold and caught in his descent the branch of another tree. There was a sharp, crackling sound; the branch snapped and Claude came tumbling to the ground, dodging by a miracle, it would appear, the weight and force of the broken branch.

John and Frank looked on in speechless amazement.

"It didn't work as well as I thought it would," said Claude in a matter-of-fact way; "but it was worth trying. I'm sorry about my pants, though: there's a tear at the knees again. It isn't such a very big one, Frank," added Claude deprecatingly.

"Pants!" bawled Frank. "It's always pants! Don't you know, sir, that there's such a thing as the tearing of limbs; that pants are a drug in the market, but that limbs lost cannot be supplied?"

> But a bold peasantry, their country's pride,
> When once destroyed can never be supplied.

answered Claude, catching at the last words of his indignant guardian.

"That fellow is possessed!" exclaimed John Winter. "After escaping with his life, he gets up and soliloquizes on the state of his breeches and tops that off with a quotation from the 'Deserted Village.' Small boys," continued this young gentleman of beardless sixteen, "weren't *quite* that bad, nor that learned, either, when I was one of them."

Frank, paying no heed to these severe reflections on times and manners, was busily brushing Claude, while that young harum-scarum made a playful feint at tickling his guardian.

"Goodness!" continued John, gazing at the two, "if an angel from Heaven were to come down and assure that young innocent that by rights he ought to have a broken leg, the boy would laugh and turn the subject off to wings or anything and wouldn't be in the least impressed."

"Well," said Frank, when he had brought the madcap to a respectable appearance, "I suppose it's no use scolding you."

"What for, Frank?"

"For the risk you ran, booby."

"Why, how did I know that that old branch was rotten? I didn't run any risk. The branch should not have broken."

"Yes," said John gravely, "the branch ran the risk, and now it's done for."

"Now, Claude," continued Frank, dismissing this last adventure with a little grimace and a gesture of hopelessness, "we're going out for a row in the sunset and we want you to come along."

"May I row?" asked Claude eagerly.

"Yes, if you behave properly."

Walking a short distance through the grove and across an open field, they came upon the near shore of Lake Vesper proper and jumped into a boat which was at Frank's disposal.

Taking the tiller ropes, Elmwood placed Claude at the stern oars, while Winter, keeping stroke with Claude, sat near the prow.

"Now," began Frank, "I want to know, Claude, what's the matter with Dockery and Pierson."

Claude laughed.

"There's something standing between them," he answered.

"Hold on!" cried Winter, dropping his oars to pull out a memorandum book and a pencil. "Just give me a minute to get down that expression. It's new to me."

Claude, nothing disconcerted, rested his oars, while Frank went on:

"What's—eh—standing between them?"

"They're singers," said Claude.

"I knew that before you came to college."

"And," continued the bow oarsman, as he endeavored to feather, "they each sang a solo at the last exhibition."

"All these things are perfectly new to us!" exclaimed Winter.

Claude had opened his mouth to add further explanations when his crude attempt at feathering brought him head first into young Winter's stomach, his little legs flying about like those of a turtle when it is thrown upon its back.

Then recovering himself with Frank's aid, he went on with his story and received no further interruptions from John, who gasped and puffed for breath as he pulled away at his oars.

"Well, the trouble is all about their solo-singing. Pierson came to me pretty blue the other day and said that he'd been told that Dockery said he sang with a face on him like a man dying of bellyache. And that same evening Dockery came and told me how he had heard that Pierson had said his voice sounded like a little girl when she sees a rat. He was mad."

"Well, what happened then?" asked Frank.

"Nothing; they didn't look at each other after that, and now when one of them wants to borrow suspenders or collar buttons or anything from the other, why, they come to me; I act as—as—"

"Go-between," said Frank.

"There's the Milwaukee boy all over!" exclaimed John. "Just as soon as he gets put out at a friend, he avoids him and goes dodging around without one word of explanation. It's so foolish. And yet I've done it myself, half a dozen times. You remember, Frank, the time I didn't speak to you for three months?"

"I should say so."

"And it was all on account of your not taking any notice of me on the street one day. If I'd gone to you like a man and asked for an explanation, I could have saved myself from being a fool. It was only when you came into class one day with a pair of eyeglasses that I began to see better."

"I began to see better, too," said Frank Elmwood with a grin.

"Then," continued John, "I asked Rob Collins what was the matter with you, and he told me that you were so near-sighted that you wouldn't notice your own mother on the other side of the street; and then, Frank, I felt so mean that I could have sold myself to the lowest bidder."

"But I was just as big a fool as you," said Frank. "I knew that you were offended about something, and I knew that I had not willingly given you any cause for offense; but I was too proud or too babyish to walk up to you like a man and ask you what you were angry about."

"Well, that taught me a lesson," continued John, "and since then I always act in the manlier fashion of asking an explanation whenever there's any appearance of a misunderstanding."

There ensued a silence; it was very quiet and very beautiful upon the water. The sun threw a golden sheen upon the mirror-like face; and above, the clouds in their courtliest colors floated serene in the dying light.

"This is an hour for poetry," Frank observed.

"Oh, that reminds me," exclaimed John; "Claude, where did you get that quotation you gave the last time you didn't succeed in breaking your neck?"

"I learnt it by heart. I know the 'Traveller' too, and a lot of Goldsmith's."

"What! Do *you* read poetry?"

"No, John; I don't think I ever read a dozen lines in my life."

"Well, how in the world do you know whole poems by heart?"

Claude laughed.

"Kate has read to me out of lots of poetry books. Whenever I like a piece, I get her to read it several times, and then I remember," said Claude simply.

"Do you know any besides Goldsmith's poems?"

"Sure! I know the 'May Queen' and the 'Charge of the Light Brigade,' and 'We are Seven,' and 'St. Agnes Eve,' and 'Ode on Intimations of Immortality,' and all of 'Evangeline,' and the 'Death of the Flowers,' and 'Autumn,' and 'Drifting,' and—"

"Stop, Stop!" cried Frank. "John, we've got an anthology with us and we didn't know it. Here, Claude, you take the tiller and I'll row."

"Now," he added, when the change had been effected, "give us the poem you like best."

Claude threw back his head, closed his eyes, opened them again, and then with a smile began:

> My soul to-day
>   Is far away
> Sailing the Vesuvian bay.
>   My winged boat,
> A bird afloat,
>   Swims round the purple peaks remote.

On he went from stanza to stanza, this harum-scarum, throwing his whole soul into the pretty word-painting of Reid's exquisite poem.

It is true he failed to bring out the dreaminess and languor of the lines; but he infused, in lieu of these, a radiancy of happiness and a brightness of life and energy which were more congenial to his age and disposition.

"Excellent!" exclaimed Frank as the minstrel came to a pause. "Now suppose you give us the 'May Queen.'"

As the boat glided slowly past Vesper Island and rounded it, Claude in his cheery voice began the poem. He was fully equal to the gayety and prattle of the first part, but as he came to the sadder portions, his interest flagged and his eyes roved restlessly about among the water lilies on the eastern side of the island. He came finally to the last two lines:

> And the wicked cease from troubling,
>   and the weary—

Here, just within three words of the sublime conclusion, Claude, dropping the tiller, reached over and made a snatch at a tempting water lily. There was a splash, a movement, and the minstrel neither weary nor restful lay floundering in the shallow water, still grasping the lily.

They pulled him in without difficulty, and Frank uttered some sharp comments.

"Well, I got that lily anyhow," was the answer.

There was nothing for it now but to return to camp with all speed, to look up more clothes for the poetical madcap.

Chapter XVII

IN WHICH IS GIVEN AN ACCOUNT OF A NOVEL FISHING EXPEDITION

THAT evening Frank called Charlie Pierson and Dan Dockery into the tent, and he noticed with suppressed amusement how carefully the two guarded against meeting each other's eyes.

"Charlie, did you ever say that Dan sang like a little girl screaming when she sees a rat?"

"No, sir," exclaimed Charlie indignantly.

"And, Dan, did you say that Charlie when he sang looked like a man dying of colic?"

"I never said anything like it. I could listen to Charlie singing all day."

"And I," put in Charlie, "like Dan's singing best of all the singing I've heard yet."

"Now, don't you two feel foolish? Here you've been dodging each other and sulking just because somebody's been lying."

"Well, I declare!" exclaimed Charlie, "I ought to know Willie Hardy by this time."

"Me, too," said Dan.

Then their eyes met, and with one impulse they grasped hands.

"I'm a mule, Charlie," said Dan.

"I'm another, only worse," said Charlie.

"You're both a pair of ninnies," added the candid Frank. "It is worth your while learning now that people will talk and carry tales. But no matter what you hear, no matter if what they say seem true or not, don't allow tale-bearing to break up a long friendship. Life is very short, and friends are not as plentiful as blackberries. Stick to your friends through good and evil report."

Then Frank departed, whereupon Dan and Charlie emptied Master Hardy's bottle of cologne and filled it with coal oil. They then slipped a few burrs between his sheets, and having tied his prettiest shirt into a number of knots, they departed arm in arm, at peace with themselves and all the world.

Willie in the meantime was elaborately protesting to Elmwood that "it wath all a joke."

For all that, he did not seem prepared for reprisals. When he went into the tent a few minutes later and poured a few drops out of his cologne bottle upon his pink ears, he uttered an exclamation, his perennial smile vanished, and he dashed out into the open air.

Dan and Charlie were awaiting his appearance with impatience, but they looked very composed and indifferent as he approached.

"Who wath uthing my cologne?" he asked.

For answer, Dan put his handkerchief to his nose.

"Pheugh!" he said and ran away.

"Wath it you?" continued Willie, fixing an angry eye on Charlie.

"Pheugh!" cried Charlie, following his companion.

And these two friends, once they were out of sight and hearing, laughed till the tears rolled down their cheeks.

The tears came to Hardy's eyes for other reasons, as he went off in search of Frank.

"Frank," he cried, "Dan and Charlie have tholen two bottleth of my cologne!"

"It wath a joke," said Frank, taking no account of the extra bottle which Willie had thrown in.

Frank, on further investigation, discovered that Willie had told Harry Archer some remarkable things about the way in which that estimable young gentleman was spoken of at the camp. Archer, after an interview with Frank, came over and shook hands all around. When he reached Willie, he took a firm grip of that youngster's hand and squeezed it till Willie danced.

"Thtop, Harry, thtop; it wath a joke!"

"So wath this," mimicked Harry, squeezing much motion into his jocose little friend.

As a result of all this, Willie found himself an unwelcome companion to all except Claude, who regarded him as an amusing curiosity.

To cement the new ties, Frank proposed a great fishing expedition for Thursday afternoon. "We'll hire two boats from the hotel," he said. "And I'll get fifty or sixty minnows. John Winter can take charge of one boat, and I'll take the other. We'll get Rob Collins and his brother to come along, and we'll have a rousing time."

"Is Hardy to come along?" asked Charlie Pierson.

"Of course; he's to supply us with fishing stories."

It was a mirthful party that set forth on the following afternoon from Mr. Collins' boathouse.

As the boats moved out from the little bay and turned in a southwesterly direction toward "Buck Island," Charlie and Dan, who were seated beside each other and who, by way of compensation for their falling out, had practiced singing together for several hours of the preceding night, softly at first, but louder and clearer as they saw that the crew of the other boat were straining their ears, sang a duet called "Whispering Hope." It is a beautiful, tender song, one of those penetrating melodies that reaches the heart. Presently Frank made a sign, the rowers rested on their oars, and midway between Buck and Vesper Islands the two friends trilled forth the beautiful strains in an elevation born of the hour, the place and their newly cemented friendship.

Vocal music gains a new charm upon the water; and when such notes, golden and liquid, are wafted over the ripples as came from the throats of Charlie and Dan—one the leading soprano and the other the solo alto voice of Milwaukee College—the effect is indescribably beautiful.

At the end of the duet, the two singers were startled by hearing the clapping of many hands from the direction of Vesper Island, and turning, they saw a group of young seminarians standing on the eminence in front of their summer villa and forming an appreciative though unlooked-for audience.

"Give them another song," said Frank.

"We are not ready," answered Charlie. "Oh, that's a fact!" he added quickly. "Let Walter come into our boat and we'll sing a trio."

The change was effected in a trice, and presently they carolled the gay, merry notes of Shakespeare's "Under the greenwood tree," ending with the words:

> Here shall he see
> No enemy
> But winter and rough weather,
> But winter and rough weather.

During the lively movement of this pastoral, Claude jumped to his feet, and would have danced had not Rob Collins reached over and, catching the lively lad's head in the landing net, brought him tumbling into Willie's arms.

"I'll thing, too, Frank," volunteered Willie.

"What! Can you sing?"

"Sure."

"He belonged to our choir at the college," explained Dockery, "but he was put out for cutting up in the chapel."

"I didn't cut up. I wath thaying my prayerth out loud, and the choir director thought I wath talking."

"That's a whopper," said Walter.

"Well go on and sing," said Frank, brusquely.

With folded hands and eyes modestly veiled, Willie opened his pretty mouth and, in a voice marvelously sweet and accurate, sang "Sweet Spirit, Hear my Prayer."

"Good gracious!" whispered Winter, "he sings like an angel."

"Yes," answered Rob Collins, "and what's more, he looks like an angel."

"One would think butter wouldn't melt in his mouth," commented Elmwood, and added, "He's the greatest fraud on the face of the earth. If he were the one millionth part as good as he looks or sounds, he'd be the best fellow in the crowd."

All of which goes to prove that fine feathers do not make fine birds.

Much as they despised him, the boys broke into applause at the conclusion of Willie's song, while the sweet singer looked ineffably pretty and demure.

Then they resumed their oars and, pulling with an equal stroke, shortly cast anchor near a point of land on the further shore south of Buck Island.

"Some of the minnows are pretty small," Frank remarked, as he put his two hands into the minnow bucket and scooped out three tiny "shiners."

"That's all right," said Rob Collins. "The small minnows for the small boys."

"Aren't you smart!" exclaimed his brother. "It doesn't take size to make a fisherman.

When it comes to fishing, I can give you points."

Then each of the small boys had a word to say.

Frank quelled the rising storm by putting the smallest minnow on his own hook and giving the larger ones to Claude and Dan.

"What we want is fish," said Frank. "Of course, if all use big minnows, we'll very likely catch nothing, or only a few large fish, but if—"

Frank finished by pulling in a fat perch.

"Give me a little minnie, too!" cried Claude.

"Me too!" echoed Dan.

"Use what you've got," said Frank, adjusting his minnow and throwing out again.

All who baited with small minnows were kept quite busy pulling in the nibbling perch, while Claude and Dan and Walter Collins sat quietly watching their hand lines, which they had cast some forty feet toward the point.

"I'm getting tired of this fishing," said Claude, jumping to his feet and giving the boat a lurch which nearly threw him into the water.

"Down in the boat!" said Frank sharply.

Claude obeyed, and it was lucky he had been so prompt, for there was a jerk at his line and he grasped it just in time to save its being carried away.

"Whoop!" he bawled, "there's no perch about this: he's pulling like a billy goat. Get the landing net, quick!"

Hand over hand he brought his line in, and his eyes lighted up as he noticed a great commotion in the waters.

"Did you see its tail?" he shouted. "Don't talk to me about your small minnows. It's a black bass."

"Pshaw!" growled Elmwood, as he brought the net under the fish, "it's only a dogfish. They're no good."

"But they're *big!*" said Claude. "Give me another big minnie."

Claude was now well content.

Walter, who had resumed his place in the other boat, now brought in a three-pound pickerel; and so excited were all over the catch that they failed to notice the coming of a boat which was manned by four lads, the oldest of whom could not be more than seventeen, and which anchored fifty yards north of them.

"Sh!" whispered Frank, as the din grew louder; "we can't expect to catch fish in all this noise."

"Sh—sh," passed from lip to lip, and making fresh casts, all lapsed into solemn silence.

Smiling Willie was the first to notice the presence of the new fishing party.

"I wonder who thothe fellowth are," he inquired in tones that could be heard from their fishing grounds at least as far as Buck Island.

"Well, that's cheeky," came in tones no less clear from the older boy in the boat, a bright, handsome lad with a fine presence and a clear eye.

"I guess they're from Chicago," observed Rob Collins wickedly. "But I'm not sure, for I can't see their feet."*

"If those fellows," observed another of the strangers, "didn't have their hats on, we could tell, by the presence or absence of hayseed in their hair, whether they come from Milwaukee or from some civilized part of the world."

Rob Collins, Elmwood and Winter were obliged to turn their heads to conceal their laughter. The boyish retort was good.

"I wonder whether those fellows intend fishing with hooks, or do they expect the fish to jump into their boat?" This was Dock-

---

*Implying that Chicago is a backwoods town inhabited by farmers whose boots bear evidence of barnyard manure.
—*Publisher*, 2003.

ery's contribution to the conversation.

"Those fellows," observed the third strange boy, "don't seem to be catching anything. There's a young man in their boat with spectacles. Now if we were to throw an idea out, he might catch that, at least."

"I'm afraid," said Frank, "that if the young persons in that boat throw out any ideas their boat won't be very much lighter."

"And besides," added Collins, "they'll go into intellectual bankruptcy."

The strangers broke into a laugh. Evidently they were a good-natured set.

"Rob," whispered Frank, "they *have* given me an idea. Get me that pickerel of Walter's quietly, so that those fellows won't notice. Pass round the word for our crowd not to give my joke away, and we'll have some fun."

Then the roguish Frank slyly fitted the pickerel on his own hook and allowed him to swim away.

"Hey, fellows!" he then shouted, "get the landing net; I've got a splendid fish."

While the strangers looked on in unconcealed interest, Frank landed his fish amidst great artificial enthusiasm.

"It's the size of the one Claude caught," said Dockery aloud.

"That ith the fifth pickerel we've caught

in five minuth!" shouted the veracious Willie.

"If you spoil our little joke by any more of your injudicious lying," snapped Rob, "we'll put you out on a hook till you're soaked. The less you say, the better we'll get along."

"It wath a joke," simpered Willie.

"Joke!" snarled Rob. "You couldn't tell a joke from a jumping jack to save your worthless little soul."

In speaking to Willie, the boys, as the reader may have noticed, were unsparing in their words. But his lying had brought him into contempt not wholly undeserved, and besides, his feelings were not easily hurt.

"Now, Rob, you take a turn in hauling him in," said Frank. "We can let Winter catch him next, and by that time our fish will be played out."

"Gracious!" exclaimed the eldest of the outsiders when Rob had landed the pickerel, "those fellows are catching big fish right along."

"Yes," added one of his companions, "and they are all of the same size, too."

Whereupon our party had great difficulty in restraining themselves from a burst of laughter, which would have put their neighbors upon the scent.

While Winter was making the fourth catch

of this most serviceable pickerel, Rob Collins to his great joy discovered a big fish straining at his line. Two landing nets were brought into requisition, and while John recovered the poor pickerel, Rob landed a lusty four-pound black bass.

"Oh, this is glorious!" whispered Frank. "Now we'll go to work and catch that black bass three times more. Those Chicago folks will respect us before we're through."

"I say," said one of the strangers, "what do you people bait your hooks with?"

"Shoe buckles!" roared Dockery.

Frank gave Dockery a stern look. The question was a civil one, and Frank was pained at Dockery's rudeness.

"We're using 'shiners,'" Frank answered affably.

"So are we in this boat, but we've only had one bite so far, and the fish got away."

The conversation was now interrupted by Claude's crying, "Hi! Hi! I've got a monster!"

Then with the same energetic ceremonies they landed the black bass for the third time.

"The reason we're succeeding so well," said Frank courteously, "is because we've discovered a new way of fishing. It's a secret yet; but if you fellows would like to know it, call over at our camp at the further end of Linnet pond tomorrow and we'll tell you, besides giving you a share of the fish."

"Thank you," returned the spokesman.

"I'll bet this fish is as large as any we've caught yet," cried Pierson, pulling in his line. "Hurry up with that landing net before he gets away."

"Why, it's the same size!" exclaimed one of the strangers. "A while ago you fellows were hauling in pickerel, and now it's nothing but black bass."

"Black bass move in shoals, maybe," explained Frank.

"How many did you catch?"

"We caught one pickerel just before you came," answered Frank evasively, "and you've seen what we've been doing since."

"That makes four pickerel and four black bass," said the stranger. "But how about the five pickerel you caught in five minutes?"

"The fellow that said that is—is injudicious," answered Frank.

At which very moment the injudicious fellow began pulling in and brought to the gunwale of the boat a fine wall-eyed pike over five pounds in weight.

"Now," whispered Dockery, "we can work this pike on them."

"I guess not," answered Frank. "They might

begin to see where the hole in the millstone is."

"When I wath here latht year," asserted Willie, in ringing tones, "I caught a pike like thith with a five-thent fishing-line, and he weighed thirty-five pounds and a half."

"That's the stupidest lie you've told since you could talk," growled Pierson.

Willie saw that no one believed him.

"He wath very heavy anyhow, and he knocked me down with one flap of hith tail."

"Boys," said Frank, "let's make for home or this boat will be struck by lightning."

Chapter XVIII

IN WHICH CLAUDE GIVES AN EXHIBITION IN DIVING AND IS TAKEN PRISONER

ON the following morning, nothing would satisfy Claude and Willie but to go fishing again.

"I wouldn't trust you two in a boat for the world," said Frank.

"But, Frank, we don't need a boat," argued Claude: "Willie and I know a spot beyond Buck Island where it's deep near shore, and we can walk there and fish without any boat."

"Will you be sure to take good care of yourselves?"

"Oh, of course," said Claude lightly.

What idea Claude had of the meaning of "to take care of himself" it is impossible for me to say.

So the two set bravely forth, established themselves on the bank and, after two hours, had secured nothing to reward their efforts.

"Hello!" exclaimed Willie, "here cometh the thame crowd that wath fishing yesterday."

"They won't have worse luck than we've had," observed Claude. "Say, let's take a swim."

"All right," assented Willie; and throwing their lines on the bank, the two undressed and were soon disporting in the water.

"Look where they're anchored!" cried Willie presently.

Claude looked and, sounding a note of triumph, ran out of the water and, with nothing on but his swimming tights, disappeared among the trees. Willie, wondering what would happen next, proceeded to put on his clothes.

The young men in the boat had chosen for their fishing grounds a deep place very close to land. They were anchored in the shadow of a huge tree which inclined toward the waters at a sharp angle in such wise that its outer branches reached out almost over their heads.

"I hope we'll have better luck than we had last evening," said Cleary, the leader of the party.

"It can't be worse," commented Allen.

"I suggest, to begin with, that we all keep perfectly quiet," growled Graham.

"That's business," put in Reilly, the last of the party.

Then they cast in silence and waited patiently. And their patience was soon rewarded: Allen landed a fine Oswego bass within five minutes.

"Didn't you hear a strange noise just now?" whispered Allen a moment later.

"Where?" asked Graham.

"Up in that tree."

At the word there was a vigorous: "Hi! Hi! Whoop!" and straight as an arrow there flashed before their astounded eyes a white form that, with hands clasped before the head, came shooting from the tree almost directly over their boat into the water with a great splash.

"Well, that beats Chicago!" exclaimed Cleary.

Claude bobbed up smiling.

"What's your luck?" he exclaimed, lying on his back and kicking his feet so as to splash the party.

"Get away from here, you little beggar!" bawled Graham. "You're spoiling our fishing."

"Oh, you needn't mind me," said Claude, striking for the shore; "I'm only going to take a few more dives off that tree."

And Claude without delay began climbing the tree with an agility which certainly astonished the discomfited fishermen.

"I never saw such cheek," said Allen.

"It's monumental," added Graham.

"So's his climbing; he's up that tree already. He's a cat or a monkey."

"Hi! Hi!" screamed Claude, springing into the air and flashing before their eyes.

"Really, boys, it paralyzes one—such coolness as that," said Allen. "Talk about Chicago! If that fellow cares about coming to live in our city, he'll own it before he comes of age.

But what an athlete he is! If I were to try to dive from that branch as he does, I'd die of fright even if I didn't get hurt otherwise."

"That's all very well," growled Cleary, rubbing away the water which Claude had just splashed into his eyes, "but we four don't intend to be made fools of by one small boy. There he goes to shore now, and he'll climb that tree again and drop on us like a bolt from the blue. Just as soon as he reaches the branch, I'll lift the anchor quietly, and when he dives, you fellows have the oars ready and we'll capture him and bring him back to the menagerie he escaped from."

When Claude emerged from the water after his third dive, he saw the oarsmen putting their oars in the rowlocks and at once made for the shore with a strong overhand stroke. But before he could reach the land, the firm hand of Allen was about his neck; and after a succession of writhings and kickings and strugglings, which inspired Allen with high respect for Claude's strength and energy, the audacious diver was a captive.

"Now, youngster," began Cleary, as he brought the wriggler into the boat, "where are your clothes?"

"Down there," said Claude, pointing toward gentle Willie, who, with staring eyes, was taking in the plight of his companion. Claude as he spoke gave a fresh wriggle and nearly succeeded in getting over the side of the boat.

"Did any of you fellows ever catch eels?" asked Cleary.

"I've caught them often," said Reilly.

"Well, come down here and hold this fellow. He's worse than any eel."

"I give up," said Claude, in his matter-of-fact way, "till you bring me my clothes."

Cleary looked into his eyes. "I believe you," he said; and releasing his hold, he turned the boat toward the spot where stood Master Willie, whereupon that faithful friend took to his heels, only stopping at the house of Mr. Collins to state that Claude had been half-drowned by a lot of roughs and that they were now about to tar and feather him. Then he made on to tell Elmwood how Claude, when he last saw him, had been screaming "Help! Murder!" at the top of his voice.

On reaching shore, Claude hurried into his clothes, which he had left at the foot of a tree. Bending down he finally put on his stockings, then with a leap he caught one of the branches and swung himself up out of reach before a single one of his guards could reach him.

"Do you intend to wait?" he inquired, grinning down at them.

Cleary looked at Graham, then both burst into a roar of laughter.

"Young one," said Cleary, "we surrender."

Claude laughed.

"Let's all be friends," he said.

"That's a bargain. Tell us who you are."

"I'm Claude Lightfoot from Milwaukee, and I go to Milwaukee College." Claude, as he spoke, leaped easily to the ground.

"Did you get all your cheek there?"

"No, I brought that along. Here, shake hands."

And Claude saluted each one in the American way with great gravity.

"I want to say one thing, Lightfoot," said Cleary. "This thing has turned out well for you. But it's a dangerous thing sometimes for small boys to take such liberties as you have taken. You might have fallen upon a hard crowd, and they would have injured you."

Claude was puzzled. The little fellow, beyond the cruel experience he had had with Worden, knew nothing of the world or its wickedness. His life had been cast in an atmosphere of innocence, and the readings

Katie had selected for him were all of lofty ideals and noble deeds. The term "bad company" and its danger had no real meaning for him. He knew his own faults, failings and sins; he did not realize that others were far worse than himself. As regards Willie Hardy, he had first been staggered but had finally come to the conclusion that as soon as Willie opened his mouth to speak, he ceased to be responsible. The world took on roseate hues to this happy-go-lucky.

It transpired in the course of the conversation that the four Chicago boys were attending a Catholic college of that city, and Claude had quite ingratiated himself into their favor, when behold! with baseball bats and walking canes, and the heaviest joint of a fishing pole, Frank, John, Rob Collins, Pierson and Dockery came racing down upon them.

"Hallo!" cried Frank, checking himself suddenly, "I thought we were on a scalping tour, and it looks more like smoking the pipe of peace. Where are the tar and feathers!"

"*Dii Immortales!*" shouted Rob, "that young perfume box has undone us again. I thought he was telling the truth this time, for when he spoke to me the tears were standing in his eyes."

"When we get back, we'll tar and feather him," said Frank. "Claude, who are your friends?"

Bats and fish poles and walking sticks were thrown aside, and the rival parties were soon on the most friendly footing.

"I hope we didn't offend you by our conduct last evening," said Frank.

"Not at all," answered Reilly, "we began the chaffing ourselves."

"No, you didn't," said Rob. "That wretched little perfume box began it all."

"Yes," assented Frank, "and when one of you made some remark about our cheek, we had to keep it up. But now you must come over and help us out with our fish."

"That's a fact," said Graham; "you fellows can't begin to eat eight big fish."

Whereupon there was a roar, and as the party moved toward camp, Frank explained his secret.

"Well, that's one on Chicago!" said Reilly.

Willie, all smiles and bows, was awaiting them. I dare not chronicle the animadversions which his companions passed upon him. But Willie's cheeks lost not their color nor his eyes their brightness, as he responded over and over, "It wath a joke."

Chapter XIX

IN WHICH KATE BRINGS CLAUDE JOYFUL NEWS

O N Saturday at noon Rob Collins presented himself at the tent with two letters which he had brought from the village that morning. One was for Claude, the other for Willie.

Claude ran his eyes over the note, then jumped into the air and knocked his heels together three times, after which he turned a back handspring.

"Kate's coming out this afternoon, and she's going to stay over Sunday with Mrs. Collins."

On making this announcement he twirled about and spun himself round and round, till he fell through dizziness.

Willie, meantime, was spelling out a card which he had taken from its envelope.

"What ith this word, Frank?" he asked, going over to Elmwood.

Frank took the card, ran his eyes over it, and then laughed so heartily as to bring the whole crowd to his side.

"Listen, boys," he said, "it's too good":

SODALITY OF ANANIAS
OFFICE OF THE IRREVEREND DIRECTOR
July, 188—

BROTHER WILLIAM HARDY: At a yearly handing in of reports it was discovered that you were equipped above all Milwaukee boys for beating the record of Ananias; whereupon you were honorably elected a member of the Ananias Company, with the privilege of having your statements of a more interesting character printed at our office for nothing.

Yours,
IT'S AN ACTUAL FACT.

Willie looked puzzled.

"Who wath Ananias, Frank?"

"He was a man who died very suddenly, my young friend, when he was making the same kind of an endeavor as you generally make to tell the truth."

Willie asked a great many questions and, on the whole, seemed to be flattered by the notice taken of him by the Ananias Society.

"It's no use trying to play a joke on him," said Dockery in an aside to Pierson. "I lost half an hour writing that note."

"Not that kind of a joke, anyhow," returned Charlie. "I really believe if a society of liars did exist, Willie would pay hard money to become a member."

This statement reached Willie's ears. He smiled sweetly and surveyed himself in his pocket looking glass.

I dare not attempt to describe the joyful meeting between Kate and Claude at the station that afternoon; what love beamed in their faces as, after the first salutation, they gazed long and earnestly into each other's innocent eyes.

I have said that Claude was in the habit of going to bed with the sun. On this day he departed from his custom, and the silver spray fell from his oar as he rowed Kate about the lake, upon the bosom of which rested the witchery of the moonlight.

Claude had much to tell that evening of his "tumbles and childish escapes," and he had a sympathetic listener. He related to Kate several things that I have not ventured to set down. Claude's temper had got the better of him several times, and I have not had the heart to picture him in his worst moments.

Kate, in her turn, had much to tell. Best of all, she brought word from their father that Claude was to make his First Communion on the coming fifteenth of August.

A great joy came over Claude's face at the announcement, which suddenly changed to an expression of fear.

"Oh, Kate! It seems so near; and I've been forgetting."

"It's not a bit too near, Claude," said Kate firmly. "You need the grace of the Sacrament to strengthen you. If you do your best,

God will do the rest."

And then to inspire confidence into her brother, she went on to tell him how St. Francis de Sales, one of the sweetest characters of history, had naturally been of high temper, yet, aided by grace, had come to a reach of meekness that was almost unbelievable.

It was near midnight when Kate and Claude before parting for the night knelt together in the house of Mr. Collins and, with a new fervor, said their night prayers, not forgetting to petition God most earnestly to dispose the little heart for the great day.

But Claude and Kate did not know the future. The fifteenth of August was not the time that God had appointed.

Chapter XX

FATHER BARRY'S STORY

"SAY, Father Barry, it's pretty hard to prove that there's a personal devil, isn't it?"

Such was the remark made by Rob Collins to Father Barry, an old and intimate friend of Rob's father, and now on a week's visit at Mr. Collins' villa. Father Barry was a priest fairly advanced in middle life and, if appearances go for anything, a genial, whole-souled gentleman. He was sitting on the portico facing the lake and watching the waters dancing in a golden and purple glow to the tender touch of the evening breeze.

At the question, the priest smiled, shifted his position in his chair, and said:

"That reminds me of a story—"

Before he could finish his sentence, Rob gave a whoop.

"Hey, fellows!" he shouted, "Father Barry's going to tell us a story."

Very close to the edge of the lake where the sloping lawn merged into the level beach, the smaller boys were engaged in the exhilarating game of Bom Bay, while Elmwood and Winter stood chatting beside them. When the word *story* smote their ears, Charlie Pierson, just in the act of clearing the pyramid of hats piled upon the patient back of Dockery, who happened to be "down," lost control of himself and alighted squarely upon Dan's back in such wise that hats and boys came tumbling unceremoniously to the earth. When the two arose, they were alone, for the others had already scampered up the grassy slope and were now grouping themselves, not without much pushing and squeezing, about his reverence. Before they had quite settled this question of precedence, the two tumblers, breathless and panting, made their presence known by their elbows, while Father Barry, flattered no doubt by the effects of the magnetism that had gone out from him, sat back in his chair and smiled. It was a captivating smile—and very patient.

"Is it a ghost story, Father?" queried Harry Archer.

"It's better than that," broke in Rob. "It's a *devil* story."

"Go on," "Go ahead," "Oh, Father, *please*—" A litany of entreaties was at once directed at his smiling reverence.

"To begin with," said Father Barry, "I never told this story to anyone before."

He paused.

"Oh, go on, Father!" cried the chorus.

"In the second place, there's not a single man on the face of the earth knows it except myself."

"Is it true?" asked Willie Hardy earnestly.

"Yes: every word of it. I've been aching to tell this story for years, and yet, up to last week, I couldn't make up my mind to do so. But now I think that it can be told safely and completely.

"Well, some fifteen years ago, I was ordained priest. Dear me! I was a handsome fellow then."

Father Barry paused, and there was a humorous twinkle in his eye.

"You must have changed awfully since that time, Father," observed Rob demurely.

"Oh, go on, Father," put in Dan Dockery; "we don't care how handsome you were then: you're as handsome now as you've any right to be."

"Well, after being ordained, I went home to spend a week with my parents and to say Mass at the church I had attended as a boy. I wasn't idle during that week, I assure you. On leaving my home, I was to take the position assigned me by my bishop in a country parish in—well, no matter where; it was in one of the Eastern States, and if I were to name it, you Western boys wouldn't know where it was anyhow."

"Oh—ah!" came the derisive comment.

"I was saying that I wasn't idle, when you boys interrupted me with your sarcastic interjections. You see, I would have to hear Confessions just as soon as I reached my parish, and I was busy reviewing my Moral Theology."

"Moral Theology!" echoed Harry Collins. "What's that?"

"It's a new patented bicycle," snarled Rob. "Why can't you let Father Barry go on?"

"Moral Theology," resumed the priest affably, "is a treatise on the way to hear Confessions. Just as a lawyer must take a course of law before he can go into a law court, so a priest must take a course of Moral, so as to know how to deal with, how to guide those who come to him as penitents: and I can assure you, my boys, that it's a very serious matter. So, then, I reviewed my Moral carefully; and then on the first Friday morning in the month of August, I took the train that was to bring me to my new field of labors. I put my valise beside me on the seat as the train started off, took out my breviary, examined my pocket to make sure that my faculties were there—"

"Most people carry their faculties in their heads," observed Rob, who would risk his life to perpetrate a pun.

"Sh!" exclaimed Harry and Walter, happily too tender in their years and development to relish the villanies of a play upon words.

"When I spoke of my faculties," pursued

the unruffled narrator, "I did not refer to those which flow from the soul, but from my bishop. Faculties, my children, is a term used in sacerdotal circles—"

"Whew!" Harry and James interpolated.

"Meaning the permission and right to hear Confessions. Only the bishop may give faculties, and without them a priest is only a Mass priest."

"Hasn't every priest the power to hear Confessions by virtue of his Ordination?" queried John Winter.

"Yes, he has the *power,* but not the *exercise* of it. Just as a man with a hundred dollars in the bank at interest has the ownership, but not the use of the money. But that's nothing to do with my story. Well, as I was saying, I made sure that I had my faculties, then opening my breviary, I said my little hours."

"What's—" began Willie Hardy.

"Oh, say," growled John Winter, "I propose that we head off all this questioning. Rob, let's you and me be a vigilance committee. Now the first fellow that interrupts Father Barry again will be run off the premises. Go on, Father."

"Umph!" growled Harry and Walter and Willie, who looked upon John's remarks as being too personal.

"As I had nothing particular to do, and besides, as I wasn't quite at home with my breviary as yet, I took a very long time finishing, and when I closed my book and, according to a little practice of mine, said a short prayer for the dying sinners of the day, and another short prayer for those little ones of God who are in imminent danger of falling into mortal sin for the first time that very day—after all this, I say, I was over at least thirty miles of my seven hours' journey, and it was hard upon ten o'clock. When I raised my eyes, then, from my breviary—now I'm coming to the story—I saw a boy leaning against the door of the car with his eyes fixed upon me in the most wistful manner. The one short glance I gave him served me to take in almost every detail of his appearance.

"He was the handsomest boy I ever saw. I am aware that I'm addressing a crowd of mamas' darlings who think they're nothing if not handsome."

"That's what!" said Rob.

"Sure!" added Winter.

"And so they are; yet, all the same, none of you come up to the boy whose eyes, fifteen years ago, were turned wistfully upon me.

"He was as handsome a lad as I had ever seen. He was about fifteen, undersized for his years, and looking much younger. A shock of chestnut hair peeped out from under his fishing hat and served to accentuate the striking beauty of his features. His eyes were full of expression and sweetness and innocence. He was well proportioned, and even in rough outing dress one could see that in him health and goodness and beauty were all combined.

"I said that his eyes were expressive, sweet and innocent. The expressiveness, as I gazed upon him, revealed trouble and sadness. Something had gone wrong with him, I could see at once.

"All this, I say, I took in at a glance: that was all the time he gave me. For as my eyes met his, a look of displeasure came suddenly upon his face, an expression of aversion from me; and he turned sharply and opened the door leading out from the car.

"'Hello!' I said in a tone that, without arousing the attention of others, would catch his ear.

"He turned toward me again and paused with his hand upon the door, his expressive face still telling me that I was an object of dislike to him.

"'Come here, my boy,' I said.

"He paused irresolutely as though some struggle were going on within him, then, evidently with an effort, released his clasp upon the door and took a step toward me. And mark this, my boys: as he let go the door and took that step, the look of aversion in his face disappeared as if by magic, and in its place came such an expression of trustfulness that I could hardly believe my eyes. Indeed, I rubbed them earnestly.

"'O Father!' he exclaimed, holding out his hand to clasp mine—and his voice was as sweet as his character, 'thank God that you called me. I was never in such trouble in my life: and if I had gone away that time—and I should have gone away had you not called me—something awful might have happened.'

"'Sit down, my boy,' I said, 'and we'll have a talk. I saw that you were in trouble, and that's why I called you.'

"He took the seat beside me and said at once:

"'Father, I want to go to Confession.'

"'Indeed,' I answered. 'If you wait till we get to L——, I can hear you, but not till then. At present we are out of my diocese. In the meantime, my boy, you can tell me your trouble.'

"'Well, Father, it's the worst trouble of my life. To begin with, my name is Ray Sumner. I am fifteen, and have been going to a Catholic boarding school in New York these last five years. After the closing exercises of this present year, myself and two college chums travelled off into the mountains for an outing. We are just now on our way home.'

"'Where are your two friends?' I inquired.

"'They're in the next car, in the smoker, poor fellows. Two of the best boys, Father, I ever met. They stood high at college and were both in our Blessed Lady's Sodality. I've known them now for three years, and never till today did I hear them say anything or see them do anything that was really bad. Of course, they had their little faults; but they were such good fellows.

"'Well, our outing passed most pleasantly. We went hunting and boating and bathing and fishing to our hearts' content. The only thing we didn't like was the fact that there was no Catholic church within thirty miles of us. It was partly, I should say chiefly, on that account that we broke up camp yesterday morning. You see, Father, I was making the Nine First Fridays, and today was to have been my ninth. The other two finished theirs on the first Friday of July. We reached the village of S—— last night and went to the house of the parish priest. But he had been called away that very afternoon on important business and was not expected back till Saturday. He was the only priest in S——, and so we had to put off our Communion. That spoils my nine Fridays, Father; I'll have to begin over again.'

"'You mustn't take your disappointment too hard,' I said. 'You can begin over, as you say; and besides, you did everything in your power. Is this your trouble?'

"'No, sir; it's far worse. The trouble began on these cars. We took this train at seven o'clock this morning and started off pretty cheerfully, considering our disappointment. Everything went along nicely till about nine o'clock—yes, till a quarter past nine, for I happened just then to look at my watch. While I was putting it in my pocket, a man stepped over to where we were sitting and said: "Here, youngsters, you must be pretty dry; we're going to have some fun in this smoker, and you fellows have got to join in." He held a bottle toward us. Now, Father, there wasn't one of us that ever touched liquor. We didn't care for it, and we always held that it was not a nice thing for youngsters like ourselves to drink, especially in public. And still, when that man held the bottle toward us, I almost instinctively put out my hand to take it; I don't know why. There was something about the color of that liquor which seemed to—to captivate me— that's the only word I can think of that comes near expressing the feeling I had. I drew back my hand almost as soon as I put it forward. But I didn't have to explain my change of purpose, for Harry Berton, one of my friends, reached over, took the bottle and thanked the man, who at once hurried away. I was surprised at what Harry had done, and was still more surprised when he put the bottle to his lips and and took a drink. I could hardly believe my eyes when Walter Sherbett, our companion, took the flask eagerly and put it to his mouth. And do you know, Father, the strangest thing of all, as it seemed to me, was that I myself was *tortured* to take a share. Somehow nothing had ever seemed to me so inviting as that wretched bottle.'

"'Perhaps, Ray,' I said, 'it was the force of example.'

"The expression which came upon Ray's features showed me at once that I was mistaken. It was a look of determination, a look which convinced me that I was speaking with a boy of character.

"'No,' Ray made answer; 'it wasn't that. I've been thrown among all sorts of boys, Father, during my five years at boarding school, and I learned pretty early that if a boy wants to be good, he's got to live up to his own conscience. Of course, I knew that it was no sin to take a drink if one could stand it, though for a boy to touch strong liquor at all certainly looks bad. But what frightened me was that I was so eager to drink. And besides, there was something that seemed to warn me.'

"'Ray, that was your guardian angel,' I said; for I now thought I saw the true meaning of my little friend's story.

"'Father, I think so myself, now that the temptation is over. My two chums tried to get me to drink, and I was almost on the point of yielding. They didn't know how near I was to giving up, and they tried to force me. One of them held me, and the other put the bottle to my mouth and tried to pour the liquor down my throat.'

"'Ah,' I put in; 'that settled it, Ray, if I know you.'

"'Exactly, Father; that settled it. I became bull-headed at once, and, much as I was fascinated by that bottle, I wouldn't have touched it then for anything. Sometimes it's good to be obstinate, Father.'

"'You were firm, Ray. *They* were obstinate.'

"'Well, they got angry at me, and swore, and called me names which made my blood boil, but I was too sorry for them to say anything. It was awful to hear these dear friends of mine I had always thought to be next door to saints swearing and talking like street loafers. I tried to get the bottle away from them, and that made them drink the more. Oh, it was the awfullest half hour I ever spent. My best friends were going to ruin right under my eyes. Father, I loved those two boys as if they were my own brothers.'

"Here my little friend's voice broke. I was strongly moved myself, for though I have roughly repeated his words, I am utterly unable to give you any idea of the pathos which he put into his story. He was as affectionate as he was firm, and as firm as he was beautiful.

"'I hate to say it,' he went on, 'but at the end of half an hour my two companions were entirely changed. They were drunk, and they talked like—like devils.'

"He put his hands before his face and paused. 'Go on, my dear boy,' I said encouragingly, 'tell me all. I feel quite sure that I can help you.'

"He gave me a glance of gratitude and continued:

"'I said, Father, that they began to talk like devils. Well, the smoker itself seemed to become like the bad place itself. There were bottles in every direction, and the cursing and blaspheming and vile singing were horrid. It seems horrid now, Father, but at the time I felt tempted to listen, I felt tempted to take part. I tried to pray, but prayer had grown ugly, and everything vile and villainous had grown beautiful. It seemed to me that God wasn't near me and everything had become topsy-turvy. I became frightened, for I feared that I was about to yield and fall into mortal sin. Just then the fellow who had given us the flask broke into a song. He had a magnificent voice, and as he began, everyone grew silent, and many crowded up to the further end of the car where he was standing leaning against the water cooler, with his hat tilted back and with a bottle in his hand. His fine voice could be heard distinctly through the car. But such a song! It was vile and nasty; and yet at the moment I would have given anything to listen to it, if I dared. But I knew that it was a question of keeping my soul white, and I made up my mind to leave the car till it was over.'

"'God bless you, my boy,' I said; for his way of speaking convinced me that he had escaped free from a general tragedy of souls.

"'My two friends, just as soon as the song began, crowded forward eagerly to hear it. They left behind them that vile bottle. Here it is.'

"He drew from his bosom a pint flask which was nearly empty. You can imagine, boys, the effect of so much liquor on lads who had never before touched it. I took the bottle and threw it out of the open window.

"'Porter,' I said to the attendant negro, who was just passing our seat, 'is the state-room of this car engaged?' He answered that it was not. I secured it at once for half a day, for I felt that I should have need of it.

"'Well, Ray,' I resumed, 'you may thank God sincerely that you have come off so well from this temptation. It was an unusual, a terrible one; and to show you that I under-stand your case, I'm going to finish your story myself.'

"Ray gazed at me in wonder.

"'When you left that vile smoker, Ray, you came into this car. At once your eyes lighted upon me, and you felt an inclination to address me.'

"'Yes, sir; that was it exactly,' said Ray.

"'On the other hand,' I continued, 'you felt an impulse just in the other direction, to get as far away from me as possible.'

"'How in the world, Father, did you know that?'

"'And another thing: the inclination to go away from me was stormy, disturbing, disquieting—in a word, just like the inclination you felt toward taking that drink.'

"'Father, Father!' cried Ray, 'you are reading my heart.'

"'No, my boy,' I answered; 'but some centuries ago there was a saint named Ignatius who wrote some rules to help us to tell the motions of the good and the motions of the bad spirit. You have had a good Angel, quiet and gentle in his suggestions, helping you against the Prince of Darkness. But I haven't finished your story yet. While you stood looking at me and hesitating, I finished saying my office and said a prayer for you—'

"'For me, Father?'

"'Yes, my boy; I said a little prayer for all the boys in the world who were that day to be tempted to commit mortal sin.'

"Ray seized my hand, while his eyes spoke intense gratitude.

"'Then I looked up, and my eyes caught yours. As soon as you saw my face, you at once were seized with a strong dislike for me—an unaccountable aversion; and while you felt moved to come near me anyhow, you were urged yet more violently to leave the car. You yielded to this feeling and started to go out, when you heard me calling you. Then the struggle was renewed, and it was with the greatest difficulty that you made up your mind to come to me and to tell me your whole story. But just as soon as you arrived at this decision you felt like your old self—am I not right?'

"'Yes, Father; but how in the world *can* you know this?'

"'As soon as you made up your mind, your feelings of disgust for prayer, the allurements of all the wrongdoing going on in the smoker vanished into thin air. You felt no longer any dislike toward me—in a word, all your temptations and evil inclinations were gone.'

"Ray gazed upon me as though I were a mind-reader. I saw in that gaze that I had told his story aright."

At this point of Father Barry's story Rob could contain himself no longer.

"Father Barry," he broke in, "excuse me for interrupting, but I am like Ray: I can't for the life of me see how you could know all that without being told."

Father Barry smiled.

"I knew the rest of his story, Rob, by inference. First of all, it seemed clear to me that the strong and sudden inclination for drink which came upon these boys was neither natural nor acquired. I reasoned that the devil was trying to put liquor into their mouths to addle if not to steal away their brains."

"Does the devil tempt people to drink?" asked Harry.

"Let me answer your question indirectly, my boy. When I first went to the seminary, I was a great smoker—"

"If anyone asks what's a seminary," said John Winter, in a stage whisper to the boys, "I'll shoot him."

"But," continued the priest, "I was obliged, as a seminarian, to lay aside my pipe and cigar. It was a little hard at first, but by degrees I became pretty well used to it. One morning, after six weeks in the seminary, I woke up with a burning desire for a smoke. During the Mass my thoughts were wandering to the imaginary fumes of a Havana; during studies my fancy was tracing rings and clouds. It seemed to me then that there was nothing in the world like a good smoke. So engrossed was I by this longing that I could hardly apply myself to my books. I felt thoroughly ashamed of myself, but there was the longing. It went to bed with me, and got up with me in the morning. It followed me, it clung to me, it haunted me. The third day it was the same. The fourth day it was worse. Then I screwed up my courage and went to my spiritual director, hoping in my heart that, after the shame of telling my story, he might let me smoke a cigar. I told him my story. He was a saintly old man of deep experience, and when I had ended, he said: 'My dear brother, what you tell me is a very good sign. The devil, when he is afraid to attack a man openly, because he sees that the man is in horror of all sin, attacks him in what he finds weakest. Your weak point, the devil thinks, is smoking. He wants to worry you about smoking, and then gradually lead you on to something worse. But you have already inflicted on the devil the strongest blow. He hates the light. You have told on him.' Then, my boys, I walked out of that room with no more longing for smoking than I had for the study of Hebrew. Now do you understand how I could infer the rest of Ray's story?"

"Oh!" exclaimed Rob, "as soon as Ray made

up his mind to tell you his temptation, the devil turned tail."

"That's exactly what happened, as I firmly believe," answered Father Barry. "The Prince of Darkness doesn't like to have his plans brought to light, and that's why he hates the confessional."

"This is all very fine," broke in Willie Hardy, "but let us hear the story."

"All right, Willie. Well, we were now travelling in my diocese, and after a few words on my part, and a short preparation on Ray's, I heard the boy's Confession—a General Confession of his whole life, in the stateroom which I had engaged. Now, I don't want to shock you boys—you know how binding on priests are the secrets of Confession. But I shall presently explain why I now say to you that this boy, whose Confession was the first I ever heard, had never in his whole life committed a single mortal sin. He had had his temptations, trying ones, too; for he carried about him, my friends, this muddy vesture of decay; but he had come off bravely, and his greatest triumph, the triumph of grace, he had won on that very morning. But a few minutes had elapsed after his Confession, and Ray was still making a short thanksgiving for the grace of the Sacrament, when the door of the car opened and two boys, both larger than Ray and a year or two older, staggered in. Their faces were flushed, and they glanced eagerly about the car. They looked angry, and I at once inferred that they had come to settle with Ray for making off with their flask.

"'Ray,' I said, 'show yourself at the door and call them here. Say nothing about me.'

"Ray did as I had directed him. The two advanced at once and, staggering into our stateroom, began to upbraid Ray in very unbecoming language. Ray interrupted them.

"'Boys,' he said, 'there's a Catholic priest here.'

"The two would have gone out, but I barred their progress."

"'Let me out,' said one. 'I'll not stay here.'

"'But you shall,' I answered. 'Neither of you boys shall leave this room till you are perfectly sober. Ray, go out and call the porter.'

"Ray made haste to obey me.

"The two wore an ugly look. I saw that they were determined to get out, even should it be necessary for them to use violence; but I was resolved to save these poor fellows, if possible, from further excess.

"One of them had put his hand upon my

shoulder with the intention of thrusting me aside when Ray returned with the porter.

"'Porter,' I said, slipping a dollar into his hand, 'I want these two young friends of mine to stay in here for a few hours till they're all right.'

"The porter gave me an intelligent nod.

"'See heah, you boys: ef either of yous steps a foot out o' dis heah compahtment, I'll git the conductah and the brakemen on you' necks!' And the porter frowned horribly.

"Boys, in general, stand in awe of railroad officials: and my two captives, even in their present condition, were no exceptions to the rule. With very ugly words upon their lips, they threw themselves upon one of the sofas and glared at me vindictively. But the porter's aid did not cease here. He came in presently with a plentiful supply of cold water and other restoratives; and despite the growling of the prisoners, he worked at them vigorously so that, with my assistance and Ray's, he soon had them on a fair way to complete recovery.

"They ceased growling very shortly, and the only signs of their dissipation were their inflamed faces and their stupid expressions. What the porter gave them then, I don't know to this day. Whatever it was, they were soon buried in a heavy sleep.

"'Now, sah,' remarked this sagacious negro, 'ef you lets them young gemmen sleep for about two houahs, they'll be jist as good as new.'

"I replied with a fifty-cent piece and wished internally that I could spare more. Ray seemed to divine my wish, for he came forward with an additional tip. The smile the negro returned us was fully worth the money. He told us to rely on him for anything we wanted, and departed with his very best bow.

"Toward one o'clock, Walter Sherbett awoke. His first words were apologies to me for his conduct. He tried to be pleasant, but he was gloomy, ill at ease, and worst of all, I could see that he held me in aversion. At all events, he was sober.

"Half an hour later Harry opened his eyes, and the same scene was repeated. Both of them, I saw, would be far happier could they escape my presence.

"And now I made a bold move.

"'Boys,' I said, 'I want you to go to Confession.'

"You should have seen their faces. Both protested that it was impossible, out of the question; and I never saw two boys more determined. But I too was in earnest: it was a fight for souls, and, as I believed, I had the Sacred Heart on my side. You know Our Lord has promised that priests who practice devotion to His Heart shall have the power of moving the hardest sinners. I had earnestly endeavored during my five years in the seminary to practice this devotion, and now I counted upon seeing the promise fulfilled.

"And sure enough, after a long discussion—how it came about seems miraculous—I persuaded both boys to make their Confession. When they had finished, they had no words to express their gratitude to me: they said they didn't understand how it was that they had been so determined not to go to Confession, and they protested that while they were still heartily ashamed of themselves and sorry for their disgraceful behavior, they were now very happy. In short, they became my warm friends, promised to write to me, secured my address and did everything within the inventive ingenuity of boys to show me their regard.

"I explained to them my theory of their day's adventures; they readily agreed with me that the bad angel had been very active, and in two cases out of the three very successful with them. But clever as I thought myself, my young friends, I was blind. I thought I saw everything. I had seen only the fact: I did not see the reason."

Father Barry paused: but there was no smile on his face.

"What was it you didn't see, Father?"

"We'll come to that, Rob. Well, when we reached my station, I got off, accompanied by as hearty farewells as ever followed a traveller.

"I see them yet, these three bright, happy boys standing upon the platform and waving their hats as long as I could follow them with my eyes. Then, trusting that they would not forget to thank our Blessed Mother, whose sodalists they were, for their deliverance, I walked up the main street and entered my church. I poured forth an ardent prayer of thanks for these three Confessions, the first fruits of my ministry. I was still engaged in prayer when I heard a great clamor without. I raised my head and listened; from out of the din I distinguished calls, in various voices, for a priest.

"Rushing up to the tabernacle, I drew out the key from my pocket and, opening the door, hastily took several consecrated Hosts from the ciborium and placed them in my pyx.

"I was tying up the bourse when a man threw open the doors of the church.

"'What's the matter?' I said. 'I am a priest.'

"There was now a sea of faces at the door, and I could hear the hearty 'Thank God' that broke from the honest lips of their owners.

"Then the man spoke, and as he spoke, the blood in my body seemed to turn to ice. Boys, do you know what had happened?

"The train I had just left had broken through a bridge four miles further up the track, and the engine and cars had been dashed down full fifty feet.

"My head was buzzing, and I was leaning for support against the altar before the man had finished his announcement. But in a moment I recovered myself and made for the door.

"A number of men came crowding about me, each one urging me to take his horse. I jumped upon the nearest and, accompanied by the man who had given me news of the accident, dashed away at full speed. It was a time of agonizing suspense for me, and fast though we went, hours seemed to be passing.

"At last we were there, and as I made my way in among dead and dying, I gave general absolution to all.

"'Father,' said an Irishman, taking off

his hat as he addressed me, 'there's a boy here who is begging so earnestly to go to Communion.'

"I followed him past faces that were set in death. Among them I saw my poor friends, Walter and Harry. They had died instantly.

"'Here he is, Father,' said the Irishman. I gazed down upon that sweet, placid face, the face of Ray—the eyes that met mine were shining with joy of welcome. Looking upon his features, one would not know that the boy's last hour had come.

"There was little time to spare. Bending beside him, I asked him to make an Act of Contrition, that I might once more give him absolution.

"'I am ready, Father,' he said, reaching his hands toward me. 'I made another Act of Contrition just before you came. What day is it, Father?'

"'Friday,' I answered.

"'Oh, thank God! Thank God!' he exclaimed, clasping his hands; 'I am going to make my Nine First Fridays after all.'

"The devotion that lighted up his face as I gave him the Blessed Sacrament was touching in the extreme; and with the memory of that sweet look of purity accompanying me like the benediction of an angel, I hurried away to attend to others.

"For half an hour my attention was wholly engrossed with the dread work of preparing men of all sorts and conditions to meet their God. Then I returned to Ray's side. The doctor had informed me that his death was imminent.

"The casualty which had wrecked so many lives was, as people then thought, a mere accident. It was only last week that I learned that it was a crime. It all came of the rivalry of two bridge builders. Mark this, boys: at nine o'clock of that very morning, two men, a bridge builder and his accomplice, had hit upon a plan for ruining the bridge—a plan that defied detection; and while these two were taking measures that would ruin the bodies of many men, the devil, who knew their nefarious scheme, was working with a last desperate effort to ruin their souls. Now you see how blind I was. I had perceived clearly that the devil was working might and main upon that train, but it had never occurred to me that there was some particular reason for his putting forth all his power of malice.

"On again reaching Ray's side, the first thing I did was to ask permission to make use, should I deem proper, of anything he had told me whether in Confession or not. He gave it very willingly. His face had grown wan, and his breathing was heavy. But he was brave and noble and joyous to the last. Not without effort, he told me how he and his two friends, seated in the stateroom I had engaged for them, had begun together the saying of the beads; how he had been moved and edified by the great and unusual devotion which marked the demeanor of Harry and Walter; how at the end of the third decade, as the two said the sweet words, 'Pray for us sinners now and at the hour of our death, amen,' there had come a great crash, and then a blank.

"After this recital Ray paused for a moment: a change came over his face, and I judged that the supreme moment was at hand. I gave him my crucifix, which he pressed tenderly to his lips and held there for quite a long time. Then, suddenly, his face lighted up with a supreme joy.

"'Father, Father,' he gasped, 'I have kept it white.'

"With a strange loveliness upon his features, he murmured the sacred Name, and still radiantly beautiful, as though his last heartthrob had been one of exquisite bliss, his face became fixed in that last tender expression of exultant love.

"Ah, thank God! Thank God! He had kept it white—I knew his meaning. He was speaking, my boys, of his robe of baptismal innocence."

Then Father Barry arose, and looking neither to right nor left, but holding his face as though he were gazing upon some vision of that other world, he walked into the house.

It was full ten minutes before the boys discovered that they were talking in whispers. Then they became silent, and upon the evening breeze came to their ears the strains from a boat crew of seminarians upon the lake as they chanted the *Ave Maris Stella* to the Queen who knows so well how to guard the purity of her young and loving clients.

Chapter XXI

IN WHICH CLAUDE TELLS A STORY

"SAY, Frank, I want to go to Confession." Claude, standing beside a hammock at ten of the night, was tugging at Frank

Elmwood's arm.

Within the tent it was very dark, so we must conclude that it was from mere force of habit that Frank reached out a hand for his spectacles and fixed them upon his modest nose before addressing the disturber of his dreams.

"Who's that?"

"It's me—it's I—it's Claude. And I want to go to Confession."

"I'm not a priest, Claude."

"I know it: but I want to go to Father Barry right off."

"Father Barry went to bed a few minutes after telling us that story, and besides, he doesn't belong to this diocese, so I doubt whether he has faculties. What do you want to go to Confession for, anyhow? You went to Father Maynard just before we left Milwaukee, and last Saturday you made your Confession to the priest in charge of the seminarians at Vesper Island. Once every two weeks ought to be often enough for a boy that hasn't made his First Communion."

"Yes, Frank, but I've been awful bad. I spoiled the fishing on those Chicago boys, and I hit Willie Hardy with all my might on the muscle so that he cried a canful of tears, and I was uncharitable because I said—"

"Hold on: I'm not a priest, I tell you. And I don't want your confession."

"Well, may I go over to the island and see the priest there?"

"At this hour of the night?"

"Yes, Frank. I did something yesterday, and now I don't know whether it was wrong or not."

Could Claude have seen Frank's face as he made this declaration, he would have seen a face made up largely of astonishment. Frank had thought that Claude was a simple scapegrace who, devoting his early years to action, had no time for thought or reflection. Now he learned for the first time that the scapegrace had a conscience both tender and scrupulous. Frank thought for a moment.

"Claude," he said at last, "your mama told you to obey me."

"Yes, Frank."

"Well now, I'm going to give you a command. Tomorrow after breakfast I'm going to the village to buy some necessaries. You may come along and go to Confession there to Father Muntsch, who's a nice, good old man. Now I order you to go to bed."

"All right, Frank. But don't you think I ought to make an Act of Con——"

"Go to bed," repeated Frank, "and don't think about Confession till tomorrow."

Three minutes later Frank arose from his hammock, drew aside a fold of the tent curtain so as to admit the moonlight and, advancing to Claude's side, gazed down upon the little face that lay bathed in the pallid splendor of the moon.

Claude was sleeping so gently and with an expression so sweet and restful upon his features that he seemed in Frank's eyes to typify the peace of God.

The picture of Tarcisius, which Claude had brought along with him and so fastened over his hammock that his eyes could dwell on it after retiring till Frank blew out the candle, was now clasped close to the sleeping child's breast.

Frank gazed at the pure, sweet face for some time; then, by an involuntary movement, his hand went to his head to remove in very reverence the hat that was not there.

Frank grinned as he caught himself in this action, and turned away.

"Well, I went bareheaded morally before that little chap, anyhow," he said, as he threw himself in his hammock. "What a beautiful soul the little scalawag must have! And I wonder why he pays such attention to that picture of Tarcisius?"

Then Frank fell asleep too.

They had a pleasant drive together the next morning. Claude was unusually quiet as, in the light buggy which Frank had borrowed for the occasion, they passed by meadows sparkling with dew upon the clover, fields of corn, and vast stretches of golden wheat. Claude's restfulness could be partly explained by the fact that he was preparing for Confession; partly, I am bound to add, by the fact that he indulged in a very prolonged lunch of bread and jam and such a number of apples and peaches as would have rendered an ordinary lad torpid and a grown man excessively ill.

Neither of these discomfits befell Claude. Indeed, had not Frank exercised his authority, the young penitent would have climbed out upon the shafts and indulged his taste in similar athletic unconventionalities.

I dare say that Claude made a very good Confession. The old village priest, a kind German, was much taken with Claude and Frank and, before hearing their Confessions, insisted on their remaining to take dinner with him.

"I don't think," Frank remarked with studied gravity, "that you'll care about having us to dinner after you have heard Claude's Confession."

"That's so," said Claude very humbly.

The priest laughed.

"Promise me now that you will take dinner with me."

The promise was given: and the good priest, whose diet was very frugal indeed, secretly ordered his housekeeper to spare neither pains nor expense in preparing a dinner for his young visitors.

Father Muntsch, I am sorry to say, took no part in this dainty repast. The dishes, piping hot, had been placed on the table, and Father Muntsch had pronounced grace, when the bell rang.

"Excuse me," said the priest, hurrying from the room. He returned quickly, having changed his cassock for a coat, and said quickly:

"An urgent sick call." Then he was gone.

"Father Muntsch," said the housekeeper, entering the room, "says that you must not wait for him: he may not be back for hours."

"I'm sorry for Father Muntsch," said Frank. "Claude, what will you take—chicken or beef, or both?"

Claude had been gazing intently for some moments at the sideboard, whereon were placed a most tempting lemon pie and some cream cakes.

"I want pie," said Claude simply.

"That's for dessert, Claude."

"I don't want any chicken, nor any beef either: I want some pie." And Claude continued to gaze wistfully at the tempting array upon the sideboard.

"Is the child sick?" asked the housekeeper.

"Sick!" exclaimed Frank. "He ought to be, but he isn't. This morning I brought along lunch for three, intending one part for myself and the other two for Claude. But Claude attended to all of it without my help."

"I'm not hungry," continued Claude, still gazing wistfully at the sideboard, "but I think I could take a little pie."

Then Claude in a businesslike way, that is, with promptness and dispatch, disposed of two quarters of the pie, and modestly called for cream cakes.

Frank, meantime, ravenously hungry after his long fast and drive, was eating the substantials.

When Claude had devoured four cream cakes, an expression of trouble again came upon his face.

"Are you sick, little boy?" inquired the housekeeper.

"Please, ma'am," said the youthful destroyer with a blush, "I think I'd like some meat and a *little* piece of chicken, if you please."

Then Frank left the room, to return a moment later with an extremely red face.

In justice to Claude, it must be said that he contented himself with a somewhat moderate proportion of the more solid foods; and thus it came to pass that before Frank had fairly begun his dinner, his brisk companion had returned thanks and was presently fingering the table in a manner that threatened a general crash.

Frank was confronted with a dilemma. To give Claude his freedom was not to be thought of. There was no knowing what astonishing feats the youngster might not undertake with the borrowed horse. The horse was wild, so was Claude. It would be a case of diamond cut diamond. On the other hand, unless Claude's attention were diverted, there was momentary danger of some catastrophe. Claude, after Confession, was wont to be intensely kittenish. How to keep Claude in order and, at the same time, take his dinner in peace was the question.

"By the way, Claude," said Frank in a burst of inspiration, "what is your favorite story?"

"The story about Tarcisius," came the

prompt reply. "*He* was a boy for you: he was brave and noble. Ray Sumner would have been like him too, I think. I wish I had Ray Sumner's picture."

"Tell me the story of Tarcisius," said Frank, as he helped himself to a piece of chicken.

"What!" piped Claude. "Do you mean to say that you don't know all about Tarcisius?"

"I will, if you tell me," was the evasive answer.

Claude arose, put his hands behind his back and, fastening his gaze upon vacuity, began in this wise:

"A true contrast to the fury and discord without was the scene within the prison. Peace, serenity, cheerfulness and joy reigned there; and the rough stone walls and vaults re-echoed to the chant of Saturday [Claude meant psalmody], in which Pancratius was the center [precentor], and in which depth called out to depth; for the prisoners in the lower dungeon responded to—"

"Hold on," broke in Frank, who had dropped his knife and fork; "are you reading out of a book?"

"I know it by heart," answered Claude.

"Well, suppose you try to tell me the story in your own words."

"All right. Well, you know, Frank, the pagans were very mean and ugly toward the Christians over in Rome; and whenever they got hold of a good man or a holy woman they got out thumbscrews, and rackets, and boiling oil, and behaved awfully. They were cruel.

"Now, once upon a time Pancratius—he was a good one!—and some others were in prison and were condemned to die by being devoured by wild beasts. The day before they were to die, a holy priest wanted to send them Holy Communion so that they could preserve the sacred Hosts overnight and go to Communion the very day they were to die. But you see, Frank, there was something standing in the way."

"What's that?" interrupted Frank.

"There was something standing in the way," repeated Claude. "That is, the persecutors had spotted all the deacons and priests in Rome, so that if any of them were to try to bring Communion to the Christians in prison, they would be taken up. So then, the holy priest, after saying Mass, was looking around for somebody who wasn't known to the persecutors to carry the Holy Communion to the prison. And while he was looking around, a little bit of a boy—Tarcisius, you know—

stepped right up and said how anxious he was to carry Our Lord to the prisoners. Do you know, Frank, I don't think that Tarcisius was as old as I am. He was a boy just like me, Frank, only he was an orphan. He was good at games, you know—"

"No, I don't," broke in Frank.

"Well, listen, then, and I'll prove it. The priest was afraid to entrust the Holy Mysteries to a little chap like Tarcisius. But when he saw what a plucky fellow Tarcisius was, he gave in. Then he wrapped up the Divine Mysteries in a linen cloth, and then put another cover over them. And little Tarcisius was so happy at the great honor shown him that he just cried, and he blushed.

"Then the priest told Tarcisius to be awful careful in guarding the Mysteries; and the little chap said, 'I will die rather than betray them.'"

Claude paused here, then added impressively: "That boy was a true American." The youthful narrator was perfectly serious.

"Well, Tarcisius got along nicely till he came to where a crowd of boys were playing some game or another. They wanted just one boy to make up their game, and when they saw Tarcisius, they were mighty glad, because, as one of them said, Tarcisius was an excellent hand at all sports. There now, Frank; that's in the book. Tarcisius used to play games just like you and me. Do you think, Frank, they played baseball in those days?"

"I believe not," returned Frank.

"Or football?"

"Not the way we play it."

"Well, I wish the man who wrote that book had told us what game those boys were going to play. Anyhow, they wanted Tarcisius to join them. But of course he wouldn't think of such a thing when he was carrying Our Lord wrapped up in the bosom of his tunic. He kept his hands pressed to his bosom, and one of the boys noticed it. Then the crowd wanted to see what he had. But the plucky little chap held on so tight that they couldn't do anything with him. They cuffed him, and kicked him, and pulled him about; but Tarcisius stood it without ever unfolding his arms. I wish I'd been there."

"What would *you* have done?"

"I'd have taken his side." Claude's eyes sparkled; he doubled his fists and brought one of them down on the table with such strength that the dishes danced.

"You'd better go on with your story," suggested Frank.

"Well, of course a big crowd began to gather at once. Did you ever notice, Frank, when you get into a fight, how quick a crowd gathers?"

"I don't get into fights, young man."

"Anyhow, there was a big crowd in less than no time, and one villain of a fellow said, 'What is it? Why, only a Christian ass bearing the Mysteries.' Then the whole crowd fell on that brave little fellow. And they were stamping on him and beating him when brave old Quadratus came up and scattered them right and left. But he was a little too late. That little boy was nearly dead. All the same, he hadn't let go of the sacred Mysteries for a single second. And so when Quadratus, who was a Christian officer, picked up that little bit of a boy, he held in his arms a mar-tyr—and—and the King of Martyrs."

Claude's face, as he spoke, glowed with enthusiasm.

"He must have felt happy, Frank, to hold two such things. You see, Tarcisius had just strength enough to tell him that he was car-rying the sacred Mysteries in his tunic, and I'll bet you anything that that big strong officer trembled all over when he took the Blessed Sacrament from the boy's bosom.

"Little Tarcisius didn't die at once, Frank. He opened his eyes a few minutes later to look upon a pagan lady who had been kind to him, and then expired. That one look converted her. You see, Frank, he was a saint. But do you know, Frank, that that brave old Quadratus made a mistake, I think."

"What was his mistake?"

"Why, when he saw that Tarcisius was dying, he should have uncovered the Blessed Eucharist and given him Communion."

"He wasn't a priest," said Frank.

"But the boy was dying, and there was no priest around," retorted Claude. "In those days of persecution, the priests couldn't always be around; and so the people were sometimes allowed to take Holy Communion themselves."

"But, perhaps," resumed Frank, "Quadratus might have thought that Tarcisius was too young."

"Too young!" bawled Claude. "If the boy had sense enough to defend the Holy Eucharist with his life, I reckon he had sense enough to receive Holy Communion too. If I was in the place of Tarcisius, I'd have asked Quadratus to give me Communion, if I was able to do it."

"But he didn't need Communion," said Frank. "A martyr goes straight to Heaven anyhow."

"You're a pretty Catholic, Frank Elmwood," said Claude disdainfully. "Every time you go to Communion you get more grace, you know; and the more grace you've got, the more you'll be able to love Our Lord when you get to Heaven."

"You are right, Claude; but Quadratus acted for the best, after all. If a thing like that were to happen in these times, it might be proper for even a layman to give Communion. But in those days the holy Mysteries were at all odds to be kept concealed from the pagans. Had Quadratus undertaken to give Tarcisius Communion, he might have exposed the Blessed Sacrament to the eyes of those who should not, according to the laws of the Church, see it, and who, once they had seen it, would have treated it with insult and sacrilegious irreverence."

"That's so," assented Claude. "I didn't see it that way before, but now you've made it as clear as daylight."

"You're not as stupid as you look," Frank was pleased to observe. "You'll be a great theologian some day."

"You needn't poke fun," retorted Claude. "Tarcisius was great. I wish—I wish—"

Here Claude, feeling that he had said too much, bounded out of the door; and before

Frank had quite finished his hearty meal, the youthful admirer of Tarcisius had succeeded in bringing about a very respectable dog fight directly in front of the rectory.

Chapter XXII

IN WHICH WILLIE HARDY ACTS AS GUIDE WITH UNFORTUNATE RESULTS, AND CLAUDE, ON BEING FOUND, MAKES THE MOST ASTOUNDING DECLARATION OF HIS LIFE

IT was nightfall. The boys were gathered about the campfire discussing Father Barry's story.

All of them, with one exception, had been singularly moved by the narration, and it had set them thinking very seriously.

"It did me as much good as a retreat," said Frank.

"I'd like to be like Ray, all my life," observed Dan.

"Maybe you wouldn't care about dying so young," said Charlie.

"Pshaw! Why not? If I could live as he did, I wouldn't care a cent when I died."

Here pretty Willie came in.

"I think Father Barryth thory wath a dreadful lie."

"Take that back!" roared Claude, his eyes flashing with rage and, advancing upon Willie with clinched fists, "take that back, or I'll knock you into the middle of next week."

Elmwood's strong arm came about the passionate little fellow's shoulders.

"Remember, Claude; remember your resolution," and as he spoke he could feel the tremblings of passion that convulsed his charge's frame.

Claude bit his lip and grew pale with anger, while Willie, who had been on the point of taking to his heels, stood off at a distance, not a little out of countenance.

"We need a horsewhip here," said Winter, staring very grimly at Willie.

"It's about time to drown that fellow," growled Dockery.

"Father Barry," explained Willie, "thaid that Ray wath prettier than any of uth. Thath's not tho," he pursued energetically, and added with charming naïveté, "I've heard folkth telling mama that I wath the prettieth boy they ever thaw. Father Barry ith a prieth, and he oughtn't to tell lieth like that."

Elmwood, still holding Claude by the arm, walked away.

"Come on, boys," said Winter, "let's go and find out the address of the nearest lunatic asylum."

Willie was left master of the campfire.

"That Claude ith a fool," he soliloquized, gazing into the fire. "He ith a bad boy too."

And Willie put on a very wise look. If this gentle falsifier had any moral sense, he kept it from the observation of the vulgar with never-failing vigilance.

Before going to bed that night, Claude called Willie aside.

"Willie, I'm sorry for the way I spoke to you. I lost my temper awfully."

"Tho you did," said Willie, who was brushing his teeth for the fifth time that day. "You wath very bad."

"I know I was," said Claude humbly. "If I can make it up in any way, I'd be glad."

Willie saw his chance. He was very anxious to supply himself with another bottle of perfume and certain articles of toilet [toiletries], which could be obtained at a village some eight miles away. He was afraid to go alone and thus far had failed in inducing any of the boys to promise him their company.

"Will you come on a big walk with me tomorrow, Claude?"

"A big walk? Sure; that is, if Frank will let us go."

"Juth wait," said Willie, as he stepped over to where Frank was reading by the light of a candle.

"Frank, I want to go to Eagle tomorrow with Claude."

"Oh, no," answered Frank. "You might get lost."

"Lotht! Why when I wath out here latht thummer for three weeks I uthed to go every day, and on thome days twith."

"Every day!" said Frank incredulously.

"Well, nearly every day. I mithed going oneth."

"Are you sure you know the roads?"

"I know them like a book."

"All right. You'd better start early and take a lunch along, for it's a good eight or nine miles. Claude can stand the walk well enough, but I don't know about yourself."

"Oneth I walked forty mileth in one day."

Frank considered it superfluous to advance any opinion on this statement. He turned to his book, and Willie departed to further the arrangements between Claude and himself.

Now Willie had been to Eagle *once*.

A word of explanation as to Claude's burst of passion. Father Barry's story had impressed him beyond any story he had ever heard. His noble heart had been touched and softened and elevated by the character of Ray Sumner. He had attributed Ray's spotlessness to frequent Communion, and he had resolved that with God's grace he would try to imitate Ray in keeping his soul white. In making this resolution, a new ardor had been enkindled within him to receive Our Lord in the Sacrament of His love. The fifteenth of August looked far away to his holy impatience. Ah! If the day were only at hand, then he would begin a new life. Ray would be his model, for he loved that gentle, firm boy, who now occupied in his mind the niche devoted to all that was high and holy and sublime.

Willie's foolish remark had fallen upon him like a blow; and, greatly to Claude's humiliation, Claude had at once burst into a fit of anger. Poor Claude! His fall made him feel still more sensibly his great need of the Food of Angels.

On the morrow, Claude and Willie started early, and after an hour's smart walking came to a fork in the road.

Willie did not remember having seen this part of the country before.

"Which one shall we take?" asked Claude, who was tripping on in advance.

"The one to the right," answered Willie promptly, "the other one goeth to Milwaukee."

And turning to the right, the pair advanced briskly.

*　　*　　*　　*　　*

Toward four in the afternoon, Frank Elmwood became somewhat anxious. The two walkers should have come back by three o'clock at the latest. They had started at seven, and allowing them the extreme limit, they should have reached Eagle at ten. They were to start for home at eleven, certainly not later than twelve, and now it was four o'clock.

He hastened over to Mr. Collins' house and communicated his fears to Rob.

"Oh, they'll take care of themselves," said Rob, endeavoring to comfort poor Frank.

"Will they?" exclaimed Frank. "Claude is one of the best little fellows in the world; but if there's any chance in his way of losing his life or breaking his legs, he's in it every time. As for Willie, there's no telling what he'll do. He's about as responsible as a cat, only he hasn't half as much conscience."

Rob considered for a moment:

"Just wait a minute," he said, "and I'll run in and ask my mother."

He returned presently and said:

"Mother feels the way you do, Frank; she doesn't trust either. She says we can take the two mares, Betsy and Virginia, and scour the country. Come on, we'll find 'em before night."

Presently the two friends were galloping down the road which Claude and Willie had taken that morning.

When they came to the crossroad, Frank said:

"Rob, you go right on to Eagle, and as you go along the road, make inquiries. If they haven't got there, come back this way and follow me."

So while Rob went on toward Eagle, Frank took the road to the left and galloped on for about two miles, when he met a man on an empty hay wagon.

"Did you see two boys of about twelve, one of them very stout and springy, the other very girlish-looking, sir?"

The man after long deliberation made answer:

"No, but I saw a girl with a big straw hat

and a tramp with a hole in his shoes."

"Much obliged," growled Frank, urging Betsy into a gallop.

Presently he came to another road at a right angle to the one he was galloping on. He paused for a moment, then adopting a cautious pace, continued straight on.

He stopped at the first farmhouse and, in answer to his inquiry, learned that a man with a black beard and a bulldog had passed by an hour ago.

A few miles further on, he came upon a sight which gladdened his heart.

In a large field, a number of farm hands were working about a threshing machine.

"Now I'll get some information," he said to himself.

Dismounting from his horse, he advanced to a group of men and repeated his question. The men compared notes and, after going over a list of vehicles and personages that had gone by, came to the conclusion that they had seen no small boys such as he had described passing that way. One of them, who appeared to be the owner of the farm, made further inquiries among the other men scattered about in various parts of the field and returned shaking his head.

"No, sir," he said, "you may rely upon it

that they didn't come this way. If they had passed, some one of the hands would have noticed them. But you look tired; let me give you a glass of whiskey, it will brace you up."

"Thank you, sir," answered Frank. "I am very tired and worried. I don't care for any whiskey, but if you've a glass of water handy I'd be much obliged."

Frank, weary and depressed, was tempted to take the whiskey, but an incident in Father Barry's story was still fresh in his mind.

"You are most welcome to the water," said the farmer. "You're the first man that wouldn't take a glass of whiskey that I've met in a long time, and I don't mind saying that I respect you for it."

Bidding the farmer a courteous farewell, Frank returned upon his tracks and galloped on without a stop till he reached the road at a right angle to his previous course. Then allowing the horse to fall into a steady trot, he said a prayer to St. Anthony.

It was nearing six o'clock when he came upon a place where the road divided at a broad angle. A saloon stood at the crossways, and fanning himself upon the stoop sat the saloon keeper.

"Did two boys pass this way today, sir?"

"Two boys of about eleven or twelve, both

of 'em handsome little fellows, and one of 'em pretty lively on his legs?"

"Yes, sir: which road did they take?"

"That one," said the saloon man, pointing to Frank's left.

"Thank you ever so much, sir," and Frank went on with a lighter heart.

But his troubles were by no means over. Roads branched in every direction on this thoroughfare, and it was only by dint of constant and careful inquiry that he was enabled to follow the young adventurers.

"They are lost sure," he said, as he changed his road for the seventh time since meeting the barkeeper.

It was nearly sundown when he came upon a lonely hut standing back a little from the wayside. He drew rein and was about to dismount when his heart gave a throb of joy as he heard Willie's voice:

"Oh, Frank, I'm tho glad; pleath take me home." And there at the door stood Willie, holding in his hand a slice of bread and butter.

"Where's Claude?"

"I'm tired almoth to death," said Willie, "and I want to get back. I'll get up behind you."

"Where's Claude?" roared Frank.

"Oh, I guess he'll get home all right. Thay,

leth start at once."

"Where's Claude?" Frank shrieked.

"He'th gone that way. When he got thith far, I wath near dead. Claude brought me in here and tried to get the woman in thith houthe to tell uth where we were. She couldn't thpeak any English, and we didn't underthand much that she thaid."

After close inquiries, Frank succeeded in eliciting the following statements:

First, that Claude had been the cause of their losing their way. (Frank knew this to be false.)

Secondly, that the German woman had succeeded in giving Claude the idea that there was a village four or five miles further down the road.

Thirdly, that Claude, bidding Willie rest in the hut till he returned from the village, where he hoped to find out where they were and, if necessary, to hire a conveyance and a driver to bring them home, had started off bravely alone.

"Stay here till I come back," said Frank curtly, and mounting his sweating mare he urged her into a gallop. Frank did not spare his mount, and before the twilight had shaded utterly into darkness, he saw the village in the distance.

Nearest him of all the houses was a modest church standing away from the body of the village by several hundred yards.

As he drew near, and with head bent forward strained his eyes to see anything that might lead to Claude's discovery, he discerned someone running down the church steps and turning, as he ran, in Frank's direction, while at the same time a pistol shot rang upon the air.

"Get up, Betsy! Get up!" he screamed, for in pursuit of the running figure came three larger forms.

"Hallo!" screamed Frank at the top of his voice. "Is that you, Claude?"

"Yes!" came the voice he knew so well.

At the sound of Frank's voice the men stopped suddenly and, turning into a field, disappeared in the gathering darkness. In a moment Claude had brought himself beside the mare. There was no smile on his face, no merry light in his eye, no healthy flush upon his cheek. He was pale, and (Frank could hardly credit his senses) looked frightened. His lips were quivering; there was a moisture that dimmed his eyes, and his little hands were folded. He looked very beautiful and very, very serious.

"Why, Claude!" exclaimed Frank, thoroughly

alarmed, "what's happened?"

Claude leaped up behind Frank, put his arms around his friend and, pillowing his face on Frank's back, said:

"Please don't ask me anything now, Frank. Give me a little time to myself; but drive away from here; and let me pray. Oh, Frank, I've just made my First Communion!"

Chapter XXIII

THE NEW TARCISIUS

WHEN Claude left Willie in the hands of the kindly but unintelligible German woman, he made bravely on to the village. After an hour's walk, it occurred to him that he had misunderstood her attempts at information. It was now drawing near the close of day, and even Claude began to feel anxious and annoyed. If the village which the woman had spoken of were a reality, it ought to be near. Claude gazed about him in quest of some point for observation. The fields on either side were quite flat; to his right rose a thick hedge which lost itself in the distance; to his left the meadows were shut off from the road and divided from each other by the common rail fence. A few hundred yards before him and just outside the hedge towered a magnificent oak tree. This tree afforded Claude the coigne of vantage which he desired. Mounting it with the skill of long practice, he straddled a branch about thirty feet above the ground and with his eyes swept the unexplored country beyond. The woman had not deceived him. A mile or so distant loomed the tapering spire of a church, and further down, the road passed through the very heart of a small village, upon whose roofs the sun was casting his parting beams.

The prospect presented to his gaze was, at that hour of the afternoon, indeed beautiful, and Claude, who was heated from his long walk, was fain to dwell longer upon it from his sheltered bower. But even as he fed his eyes upon the wide sweep of landscape before him, he remembered Frank and thought of the disquiet that his absence must be causing his guardian. He brought his legs on the same side of the branch and was about to descend, when he observed two men within a short distance of him, walking over the ground he had so lately traversed.

He paused to look at them and, strange for Claude, was unfavorably impressed. One of them was a man beyond middle age with a thick neck, heavy lips and coarse features. His face was covered with black bristles, while the hair of his head was sprinkled with gray. His companion was a thin, nervous man, young, beardless, with a pale, haggard face and a scar slanting across the upper lip. His face, though not altogether lacking in refinement, was repulsive. The two were gesticulating and talking in tones of excitement.

"Here's where we're to meet him, Delaney," said the elder man. "And it's a cool place, too," saying which he seated himself at the foot of the tree.

"He should have been here by this time, Jordan, confound him!" snarled Delaney. "We want to loot the place before the priest gets back."

"Bosh!" growled the other in a hard, metallic voice. "You've no nerve, man. The priest can't possibly get back before ten o'clock tonight. I sent him on a sick call which will give him fifteen miles' ride there alone. You just keep cool, young man."

"Do you know where everything is, Jordan?"

"Yes; I know the lay of the church pretty

well. In the room back of the altar—"

"The sacristy, you mean."

"Oh, bother the name!—there's two gold cups and one silver cup—"

"They're called chalices," put in Delaney. "I was an altar boy once."

"Then," continued Jordan, "there's a lot of lace stuff."

"Surplices, you ignoramus."

"Well, no matter; they're costly. The priest has rich relations in Germany, and they've been giving him lots of fine things. Those two gold cups came from Germany and are worth taking."

"What about the ciborium?" asked Delaney.

Claude had not moved a muscle during this conference. He listened quietly, but with a face every feature of which had sharpened into eagerness of attention.

"Ciborium!" repeated the other.

"Yes; that's kept in the tabernacle."

"Talk English!" said Jordan.

"You're a fool!" cried Delaney, the cut upon his lip quivering and giving a most forbidding expression to his face. "Didn't you see a light in the church?"

"Yes, it was burning before a sort of table."

"Before the altar, you mean. Well, right above the table, as you call it, didn't you see a sort of little house with a little door, and a keyhole in it?"

"Yes."

"Well, that's the tabernacle. Inside that there's a sort of goblet, covered with a veil of silk. The goblet maybe is of gold. If it's of silver, then the inside is gold-plated."

"Oh!" exclaimed the other with fervor, "I do hope it's of gold."

"Well, in that cup they keep a lot of little white pieces of bread called Hosts. The Catholics say that it has only the form and appearance of bread, but that in reality it is God the Son."

"I don't care what they think," grumbled the other. "But I hope the cup is of gold."

"But I do care," said Delaney, with his gashed upper lip curling so as to show his sharp white teeth. "I'll get even with 'em for making me believe that those pieces of bread were God. I'll get even with that cursed Dutch priest who prevented me from marrying a girl because I stood up for Ingersoll. I'll take every Host in that ciborium, and I'll break each one in bits, and I'll scatter them all about the church. Ugh! What a fool I was the day I made my First Communion!"

Claude turned pale as he caught these blasphemous words, and was within a little of losing his hold upon the branch. So that man below him had made his First Communion!

Jordan merely laughed.

"They say I was a pious boy," continued the other in low, scornful tones. "They meant that I was a fool. I might be a fool yet, if my father hadn't taken me from the Catholic school and sent me to finish at the high school, and stopped the Catechism business, and made my mother let up on religion. I began to see how I had been fooled. I read Ingersoll. He's my man; and I've got along first rate without the help of the Christian God."

The language was hideous, the face in keeping with the language.

"And so that man made his First Communion once upon a time," thought Claude, his face pale with horror. Then he thought of Ray, the young, the beautiful, the innocent.

"Ah! Here comes Monroe," cried Jordan, who paid no attention to Delaney's reminiscences. "Is it all right, Monroe?" he asked eagerly.

"Yes," answered Monroe, producing from his pocket a large key. "Here's the key of the church. I sent the housekeeper a message from her sister who lives six miles north of here, and she bit at once. As soon as she left I got this key."

"What about the key of the tabernacle?" asked Delaney eagerly.

"That's provided for. The priest, you know, carries the key of the tabernacle himself."

"Oh, we can smash the tabernacle," said Jordan.

"That won't be necessary," said Monroe. "There's a key hanging on a nail behind the door in the sacristy; it opens the wardrobe, but it happens to fit the tabernacle too. You see I know things pretty well."

"What else did you live in the village for?" asked Jordan.

"I'll take care of that tabernacle," said Delaney. "And it would do me good to see how the people will look when they find they've been stamping on their Hosts as they walk through the aisles."

"I didn't know I'd get this key of the church door," continued Monroe, "and so first I thought we'd have to climb through the sacristy window. It's twelve feet high; but there's a lightning rod beside it, and the window isn't bolted."

"The key is a long sight better," said Jordan.

"Well, why don't you fellows come on?" growled Delaney. "One would think that you had a week to do it in."

"Yes; but before we start, the question is how shall we go?"

"Oh, on the road of course," said Monroe.

"Won't we be seen?"

"There's next to no risk because the people are mostly all, except the sick and an old granny or so, out on a picnic; and I know for sure that they won't start back till the moon is up."

"Yes, and it will be up pretty soon!" cried Delaney nervously, "for the sun is down already. Come on."

Jordan rose.

"Now remember," he said impressively, "remember that we're not to do any running or show any signs of being in a great hurry, so that even if someone sees us, they won't think that we're up to any game. Step out now."

Claude waited till they were gone some little distance, when he quickly climbed to the end of the branch on which he had been sitting, thus bringing himself on the inner side of the hedge. Then he swung himself to a lower branch, and from that dropped to the ground, a feat that few boys could have performed without injury to their limbs. Screened by the hedge, he broke into a light trot, picking each step as he went. The crackle of a twig, the rustle of a leaf, might attract the notice of the horrible trio preceding him on the road. As he drew nearer them, he became more wary. He stepped quickly, but he chose each foothold with an unerring eye. On he moved, light as a fairy, on, till he was abreast the men, and held his breath, and wondered whether they could possibly hear the beating of his heart. Slowly, surely, he advanced; slowly, lightly, deftly, till at length the men were many paces behind. Then Claude took a long breath and broke into a run, where earnestness and energy and love and determination lent wings to the natural speed of his feet. On he dashed, perfect master of his breath, the rich color mounting into his cheeks, the breeze of the calm twilight sweeping his soft hair over his brow; on he dashed till the hedgerow ceased and a rail fence stood before him.

Not stopping even to put his hand on the fence, Claude leaped high in the air and made on, nor did he even so much as turn his head to see whether the thieves were in sight or not. Luckily a bend in the road shut him off from their sight.

Very shortly the church was gained, and Claude, grasping the lightning rod, went up hand over hand to a level with the window. It was the work of one moment to throw back the shutter and open the window, the work of another to leap into the room, snatch the key from the sacristy and hurry into the sanctuary.

It was rather dark in the church, so dark that for a moment Claude, coming out of the clearer light of the sacristy, could discern objects with difficulty. At the gospel side upon the altar rested the sanctuary lamp, its trembling flame shining through the red glass in honor of the Blessed Sacrament.

Claude made a genuflection, ascended the altar step and, fitting the key into the lock, threw open the door of the tabernacle.

As he genuflected for the second time, he could distinctly hear the beatings of his heart.

In the tabernacle there was a veiled object. Claude removed the veil, raised the cover and, holding the ciborium with trembling hands, looked down into its cup.

There lay twelve consecrated Hosts!

Imagine a man who after years of preparation and study has been ordained, ascending the altar to say his first Mass. His limbs tremble beneath him when for the first time he pronounces the sacred words of Consecration and knows that with the pronounc-

ing of these words what had been bread
before is now the Body and Blood, the Soul
and Divinity of Christ. Very similar was the
feeling of Claude as he gazed upon the sacred
Particles.

Here he stood face to face with Him who,
although Ruler of earth and sky, had been
born in a stable; with Him who had been
despised, insulted, put to death. He had conquered death, but He could still be insulted;
and it was Claude's office to save Him. And
as Claude fell upon his knees still holding
in his hands the ciborium, he turned from
Christ to himself; at once in a long endless
procession came his sins, his faults, his neg-
ligences, his bursts of anger—ah, how terrible they looked! Sins! Against whom?
Claude asked himself this question and, looking into the ciborium, saw the answer. They
were against Him who through love for us,
through the desire of being ever with us to
feed us with the Bread of Life, had for nineteen centuries borne the insults and out-
rages of thousands and thousands of brutal,
ungrateful men. And with this thought,
Claude made an Act of Contrition for the
sins of his life. All these thoughts flashed
through Claude's mind with incredible rapid-
ity. These few moments crowded together

thoughts that, in ordinary circumstances, should occupy hours. Again a fit of trembling came upon him; there were steps approaching; the awful moment was come. For Claude was determined that not one of the consecrated species should ever fall into the renegade's hands. They might take his life—that question he did not consider worth the dwelling upon. But think of it! He a small boy, who had but the night before flown into a passion, he was now to hold God in his fingers and receive Him into his bosom!

Then surging upon his soul came all his sins like waves of menace; his scrupulosity had reached the snapping point; and as he heard the footfalls of the thieves ascending the steps of the church, the scrupulosity snapped.

Bowing his head, while tears, born of many and varied emotions, started to his eyes, he murmured reverently:

"Lord, I am not worthy"; and with the words he took the Hosts in his trembling fingers and placed them in his mouth. Folding his hands in prayer, and turning upon the kneeling bench so as to face the door, he waited. Claude had made his First Communion!

The key turned in the lock and three men entered, the atheist Delaney taking the lead.

"My God!" cried the atheist, jumping back and falling against Jordan. "What's that?"

No wonder he started in terror. The church to those who had just entered out of the waning twilight was quite dark, save within the radius of a few feet of the sanctuary lamp. And there within its radius Delaney's eyes fell upon a face, fair, beautiful, sweet, composed, the calm eyes looking straight at him—blue, calm eyes and open, shining with a sweetness, a sorrow and a light such as would become an angel in human form standing guard at a desecrated shrine.

Jordan caught Delaney's hand, Monroe put his arms through Jordan's; and while Delaney would have taken to flight, the other two stood in stupid alarm. There was a silence.

But Claude! Happy Claude! Those moments of silence were the sweetest of his life. For in those fleeting seconds great waves of love flooded his soul, and great waves of light illumined his mind. He saw it now, he saw what he had failed to see in his adventure with Worden; he saw the horror and ugliness of sin. There it rose before him stamped upon the souls and faces of the men who stood in the twilight at the door. Those three men represented sin. It was possible, he perceived in that moment of insight, to be a sinner without being a thief, a profaner of the Blessed Sacrament, a murderer—but in the long run, sin was sin; and every sinner, no matter whether he were rough or gentle, high or low, rich or poor: every sinner in the world cast his lot in with these men—there might be a difference, but the difference was of degree, not of kind.

Facing him there was sin, but—ah, what a gulf between them!—next to sin, near to sin by the length of a church, was Love, Incarnate Love. There was to be a choice between these two: Sin with its foulness, Christ with His love. No reasoning creature of God's could escape the choice. And now the choice was given to Claude. In answer his soul soared high in a blaze of love. The light, the true light, was within his bosom. He saw the light, he heard the voice, and aided by the powerful graces that were finding full play of activity in his soul, he made an act of perfect love, and love drove out fear. Claude's scruples were gone forever.

And so there was sin in the world. Claude had never before appreciated this sad fact; but now in the light that poured upon him he saw the mystery of life, and upon his spirit settled a sense of the sacredness of his own being. It was given to him to use, for love consists not in words but in deeds.

All these things flashed through Claude's mind while the three men stood pausing at the door.

"It's a human being," whispered Jordan. "I saw tears on its face; it can't be a ghost."

"I thought it was an angel," said Delaney.

"Humph! I thought you didn't believe in God! Who's that?" called Jordan in a loud voice.

Claude continued to pray in silence.

"Are you a boy?" cried Monroe.

No answer.

"Well," said Jordan, "suppose we move up together."

The three stepped slowly up the middle aisle. As they advanced, Claude rose to his feet.

"Why, it's nothing but a boy!" cried Delaney. "I see his clothes now. We must catch him before we do anything else. Boy, come here."

Claude neither spoke nor moved. He was watching his chance to escape, to bring away his life which belonged to God.

With an oath, Delaney rushed at Claude. Just as he was about to put his hands upon him, Claude, who had stepped upon a kneeling bench, leaped over the altar railing into the side aisle and sprang for the door. The three were after him at once, and as he flew down the steps a bullet whistled by his ear.

Then Claude heard Frank's welcome voice. He answered at once. But it was not the same Claude whom Frank had known that made answer; for in the few minutes that had passed before the tabernacle, Claude had undergone a wondrous change and the problem had been solved.

Chapter XXIV

CONCLUSION

SHORTLY before reaching the house where young Hardy was staying, Claude, having finished his long thanksgiving, told Frank, in great simplicity of words, his strange adventure.

Frank was so moved that he was hardly able to speak. At times during the narration he glanced over his shoulder, half expecting to see the throng of radiant angels that must have made the progress of his charge along this country road sacred and sweet with their lovely attendance.

They found Rob Collins with Willie awaiting them at the house of the German woman. Speaking unconsciously in a whisper, Frank told Rob of the wondrous thing that had come to pass.

Rob glanced at Claude, whose face still gave evidence of the holy thoughts and inspirations which so recently had enjoyed full play in his radiant soul.

"Frank," said Rob in a whisper, "I remember when I was preparing for my First Communion how Father Maynard used to insist that one Communion could make a saint."

"And now," said Frank, "you understand."

Then Rob, at Frank's suggestion, rode to the village to tell the parish priest of what had happened; and Frank, having hired two horses of a farmer, brought Claude and Willie back to the camp.

It had been Frank's intention to break up camp on the afternoon of the following day. But now he resolved to hasten his preparations so as to take the early morning train for Milwaukee.

On reaching the city next morning, Claude went at once to his father's office.

"Why, Claude!" exclaimed Mr. Lightfoot,

jumping from his chair, "what brings you here?"

Claude returned his father's kiss, and then told his story.

Mr. Lightfoot was far more moved than Frank had been. The tears came to his eyes, he bowed his head to conceal his emotion, and, when Claude had come to an end, he took his little boy in his arms, kissed him tenderly and said:

"God bless you, my little child."

Then he bowed his head upon his hands again.

"Claude," he said presently, "do you think of going to Communion next Sunday?"

"I'd like to, sir, very much."

"Well, Claude, with God's help, I shall go to Communion with you." And if Claude hereupon exhibited a joy of surprise which fell just short of dancing in its expression, none of my readers should be astonished. Mr. Lightfoot had not approached the holy table for the past seven years.

As the happy father and happy son took their way homeward, Claude, after some hemming and stuttering, at length said:

"Papa, I want to ask you one question."

"Certainly, Claude."

"Do—do you think it was—American?"

The people on the streets may have been astonished somewhat at Mr. Lightfoot's answer to this simple question. Again he caught his boy up and pressed him close.

"Claude," he then said, "if you're faithful to your God, there's no danger of your being unfaithful to your country. You may go to Milwaukee College as long as you like."

And again Claude was tempted to break into a short and simple dance of his own composition.

"I have noticed," continued Mr. Lightfoot, "that there have been many men untrue to their religion and untrue to their country at the same time, but I don't know of a single case in which a man living as a true Christian ever betrayed his native land."

The reader may imagine the joyous meeting between Claude and his mother.

*   *   *   *   *

Three months ago, Claude had been wild, impetuous and passionate. He had threatened to become ungovernable. Recklessness and a high temper, when they join forces, may bring about dire results. Frank Elmwood, in his first moments of acquaintance with Claude, had read the youngster's character and been puzzled by the problem. The solution had come about in a few minutes. And it had come from Heaven.

Claude, from the moment he made his First Communion, was a changed boy. And yet, in another sense, he is the same Claude. His smile is as genial, his laugh is as light, his limbs are as quick as when we first made acquaintance with the dancing sunbeam. He is different in that he has been taught in one sharp yet sweet lesson of divine grace to reflect, to think: to keep in mind that he is a responsible being. In class, he is a model of behavior; at home, he is an earnest student; in the playground, he is the leader of all his fellows; and everywhere, he is happy as the day is long. As indeed is very natural, he misses Kate, who is finishing her studies at the Visitation Convent in St. Louis. It is possible that Claude will continue to miss her for years to come; for Kate, charmed by the high ideal which the rule of the Visitandines presents, and drawn by the modesty, holiness and charity of those gentle ladies who live so sweetly and graciously the same hidden life that gave us a Blessed Margaret Mary, has already made application to be received into their ranks. And Claude is indeed pleased with his sister's choice. Of course, he will miss her at times. But he will not suffer from lonesomeness. Claude, at the present writing, has a little brother two years of age; and I am given to understand by Mrs. Lightfoot's lady friends, who appear to be experts in such matters, that a finer child than Frankie Elmwood Lightfoot never opened his eyes upon the delightful city of Milwaukee. If one can judge by Claude's attentions to the infant, he too is of the same opinion. Mrs. Lightfoot, I am glad to say, is no longer an invalid. On the very day that Claude, under such startling circumstances, made his First Communion, his mother experienced a decided change for the better; and she maintains to this hour that it was the fervent prayers of her dear little boy which brought about this change.

Claude still cherishes the picture of Tarcisius. Whenever he looks at it, he thinks of his First Communion and wonders whether he shall ever again feel so unspeakably happy in this world.

Who knows? Should Claude, in the years to come, ascend the altar some day as the *legitimate* minister of the Blessed Sacrament, I dare say that his heart, kept pure and spotless, let us hope, by the singular graces of God, shall throb at the awful words of Consecration with a bliss even more unspeakable than the bliss with which it throbbed when he made that memorable First Communion by which the problem was solved.

THE END

If you have enjoyed this book, consider making your next selection from among the following . . .

Prices subject to change.

Prices subject to change.

Catholic Home Schooling. *Mary Kay Clark* 21.00
Forty Dreams of St. John Bosco. *Bosco* 15.00
Story of a Soul. *St. Therese of Lisieux* 9.00
Catholic Dictionary. *Attwater* 24.00
Catholic Children's Treasure Box Books 1-10 . . . . 50.00
Prayers and Heavenly Promises. *Cruz*. 6.00
Magnificent Prayers. *St. Bridget of Sweden* 2.00
The Happiness of Heaven. *Fr. J. Boudreau* 10.00
The Glories of Mary. *St. Alphonsus Liguori* 21.00
The Curé D'Ars. *Abbé Francis Trochu* 24.00
Humility of Heart. *Fr. Cajetan da Bergamo* 9.00
Love, Peace and Joy. (St. Gertrude). *Prévot* 8.00
Passion of Jesus & Its Hidden Meaning. *Groenings* 15.00
Mother of God & Her Glorious Feasts. *Fr. O'Laverty* . . . 15.00
Song of Songs—A Mystical Exposition. *Fr. Arintero* . . . 21.50
Love and Service of God, Infinite Love. *de la Touche* . . 15.00
Life & Work of Mother Louise Marg. *Fr. O'Connell* . . . 15.00
Martyrs of the Coliseum. *O'Reilly*. 21.00
Rhine Flows into the Tiber. *Fr. Wiltgen* 16.50
What Catholics Believe. *Fr. Lawrence Lovasik* 6.00
Who Is Therese Neumann? *Fr. Charles Carty*. 3.50
St. Francis of Paola. *Simi and Segreti* 9.00
The Rosary in Action. *John Johnson* 12.00
St. Dominic. *Sr. Mary Jean Dorcy*. 13.50
Is It a Saint's Name? *Fr. William Dunne*. 3.00
St. Martin de Porres. *Giuliana Cavallini* 15.00
Douay-Rheims New Testament. *Paperbound* 16.50
St. Catherine of Siena. *Alice Curtayne* 16.50
Blessed Virgin Mary. *Liguori* 7.50
Chats With Converts. *Fr. M. D. Forrest* 13.50
The Stigmata and Modern Science. *Fr. Charles Carty*. . . 2.50
St. Gertrude the Great 2.50
Thirty Favorite Novenas 1.50
Brief Life of Christ. *Fr. Rumble* 3.50
Catechism of Mental Prayer. *Msgr. Simler* 3.00
On Freemasonry. *Pope Leo XIII* 2.50
Thoughts of the Curé D'Ars. *St. John Vianney* 3.00
Incredible Creed of Jehovah Witnesses. *Fr. Rumble* 3.00
St. Pius V—His Life, Times, Miracles. *Anderson*. 7.00
St. Dominic's Family. *Sr. Mary Jean Dorcy* 27.50
St. Rose of Lima. *Sr. Alphonsus* 16.50
Latin Grammar. *Scanlon & Scanlon* 18.00
Second Latin. *Scanlon & Scanlon* 16.50
St. Joseph of Copertino. *Pastrovicchi* 8.00

Prices subject to change.

At your Bookdealer or direct from the Publisher.
Toll Free 1-800-437-5876   ***www.tanbooks.com***

Prices subject to change.

Catholic Books for Young People

Catholic Children's Treasure Box Books 1-10 (Ages 3-8+) . . 50.00
Catholic Children's Treasure Box Books 11-20 (Ages 3-8+) . . 50.00
My Confession Book. *Sr. M. A. Welters*. (Ages 6-10) 2.00
My See and Pray Missal. *Sr. J. Therese*. (Ages 4-8) 2.00
Set of 20 Saints' Lives by Mary Fabyan Windeatt. 160.00
Children of Fatima. *Windeatt*. (Ages 10 & up) 11.00
Curé of Ars. *Windeatt*. (Ages 10 & up) 13.00
Little Flower. *Windeatt*. (Ages 10 & up) 11.00
Patron St./First Communicants. *Windeatt*. (Ages 10 & up) . . . 8.00
Miraculous Medal. *Windeatt*. (Ages 10 & up) 9.00
St. Thomas Aquinas. *Windeatt*. (Ages 10 & up) 8.00
St. Catherine of Siena. *Windeatt*. (Ages 10 & up) 7.00
St. Rose of Lima. *Windeatt*. (Ages 10 & up) 10.00
St. Benedict. *Windeatt*. (Ages 10 & up) 11.00
St. Louis De Montfort. *Windeatt*. (Ages 10 & up) 13.00
Saint Hyacinth of Poland. *Windeatt*. (Ages 10 & up) 13.00
Saint Martin de Porres. *Windeatt*. (Ages 10 & up) 10.00
Pauline Jaricot. *Windeatt*. (Ages 10 & up) 15.00
St. Paul the Apostle. *Windeatt*. (Ages 10 & up) 15.00
King David and His Songs. *Windeatt*. (Ages 10 & up) 11.00
St. Francis Solano. *Windeatt*. (Ages 10 & up) 14.00
St. John Masias. *Windeatt*. (Ages 10 & up) 11.00
Blessed Marie of New France. *Windeatt*. (Ages 10 & up) . . . 11.00
St. Margaret Mary. *Windeatt*. (Ages 10 & up) 14.00
St. Dominic. *Windeatt*. (Ages 10 & up) 11.00
Anne—Life/Ven. Anne de Guigne (1911-1922). *Benedictine Nun*. 7.00
Under Angel Wings—True Story/Young Girl & Guardian Angel. 9.00
Pope St. Pius X. *F. A. Forbes*. 11.00
Child's Bible History. *M. Rev. F. J. Knecht*. 7.00
Forty Dreams of St. John Bosco. *St. John Bosco* 15.00
Blessed Miguel Pro—20th Century Mexican Martyr. *Ann Ball* 7.50
Story of a Soul. *St. Therese*. 9.00
The Guardian Angels. 3.00
St. Maria Goretti—In Garments All Red. *Fr. G. Poage*. 7.00
The Curé of Ars—Patron Saint of Parish Priests. *Fr. O'Brien*. 7.50
St. Maximilian Kolbe—Knight of the Immaculata. *Fr. J. J. Smith*. 7.00
Life of Blessed Margaret of Castello. *Bonniwell*. 9.00
Story/Church—Her Founding/Mission/Progress. (7th-12th Grades) 22.50
Bible History. *Johnson, Hannan & Dominica*. (Grades 6-9+) . 24.00
Bible History Workbook (to accompany above). *Ignatz*. 21.00
Set: Bible History Text & Workbook. 36.00

Prices subject to change.

St. Teresa of Avila. *F. A. Forbes*. (Youth–Adult) 7.00
St. Ignatius Loyola. *F. A. Forbes*. (Youth–Adult) 7.00
St. Athanasius. *F. A. Forbes*. (Youth–Adult) 7.00
St. Vincent de Paul. *F. A. Forbes*. (Youth–Adult) 7.00
St. Catherine of Siena. *F. A. Forbes*. (Youth–Adult) 7.00
St. John Bosco—Friend of Youth. *F. A. Forbes*. (Youth–Adult) 9.00
St. Monica. *F. A. Forbes*. (Youth–Adult) 7.00
Set of 7 Saints' Lives above by F. A. Forbes. ($51.00 value) 39.00
Set of 24 Catholic Story Coloring Books. *Windeatt & Harmon* 72.00
Our Lady of Fatima Catholic Story Coloring Book. 4.50
Our Lady of Lourdes Catholic Story Coloring Book. 4.50
Our Lady of Guadalupe Catholic Story Coloring Book. 4.50
Our Lady of the Miraculous Medal Catholic Story Coloring Bk. 4.50
Our Lady of La Salette Catholic Story Coloring Book. 4.50
Our Lady of Knock Catholic Story Coloring Book. 4.50
Our Lady of Beauraing Catholic Story Coloring Book. 4.50
Our Lady of Banneux Catholic Story Coloring Book. 4.50
Our Lady of Pontmain Catholic Story Coloring Book. 4.50
Our Lady of Pellevoisin Catholic Story Coloring Book. 4.50
St. Joan of Arc Catholic Story Coloring Book. 4.50
St. Francis of Assisi Catholic Story Coloring Book. 4.50
St. Anthony of Padua Catholic Story Coloring Book. 4.50
St. Dominic Savio Catholic Story Coloring Book. 4.50
St. Pius X Catholic Story Coloring Book. 4.50
St. Teresa of Avila Catholic Story Coloring Book. 4.50
St. Philomena Catholic Story Coloring Book. 4.50
St. Maria Goretti Catholic Story Coloring Book. 4.50
St. Frances Cabrini Catholic Story Coloring Book. 4.50
St. Christopher Catholic Story Coloring Book. 4.50
St. Meinrad Catholic Story Coloring Book. 4.50
Bl. Kateri Tekakwitha Catholic Story Coloring Book. 4.50
The Rosary Catholic Story Coloring Book. 4.50
The Brown Scapular Catholic Story Coloring Book. 4.50
Christ the King—Lord of History. *Anne Carroll*. (H. S. Text). 24.00
Christ the King, Lord of History Workbook. *Mooney.*. 21.00
Set: Christ the King Text and Workbook. 36.00
Christ and the Americas. *Anne Carroll*. (High School Text). . 24.00
Old World and America. *Bishop Furlong*. (Grades 5-8). 21.00
Old World and America Answer Key. *McDevitt*. 10.00
Our Pioneers and Patriots. *Bishop Furlong*. (Grades 5-8). . . . 24.00
Our Pioneers and Patriots Answer Key. *McDevitt*. (Grades 5-8). 10.00

At your Bookdealer or direct from the Publisher.
Toll Free 1-800-437-5876   ***www.tanbooks.com***

Prices subject to change.

From the cover of Tom Playfair . . .

TOM PLAYFAIR is one of "Fr. Finn's Famous Three"—**Tom Playfair**, **Percy Wynn** and **Harry Dee**. These were the most popular of Fr. Finn's 27 Catholic novels for young people. Resembling a Catholic version of Charles Dickens' stories, or even *The Hardy Boys*, these books were read by hundreds of thousands of young people in the late 19th and early-to-mid 20th century. Their quaint turn-of-the-century language is part of the charm of the stories and of Fr. Finn's own brand of humor. After young readers (or hearers) have "gotten into" his style, they find it hilarious! But besides being fun, the stories have a moral: Tom Playfair is an unruly little boy when he is sent to St. Maure's boarding school, but he develops into a good Catholic young man and leader—without ever losing his high spirits. (All 3 books feature Tom Playfair.)

But what about today's young people?

We were given great encouragement to reprint these books by the experience of a teaching Sister who reads all 3 books each year to her 5th and 6th graders—with very gratifying results. Sister says she has seen drastic changes in students after hearing Fr. Finn's stories—marked improvement in behavior, motivation *and character*, especially in boys. Though both boys and girls enjoy the books immensely, she says, "It's the boys that absolutely love them. It's a hero worship thing." And parents ask: "Who's this Tom Playfair?—because that's all the kids talk about at the dinner table on Monday nights."

Grade level: 5ᵗʰ-8ᵗʰ (and older!)

Tom Playfair was "the most successful book for Catholic boys and girls ever published in the English language." —Benziger Brothers Publishers

Perfect for reading aloud at home or at school! Great for book reports! Include an "About the Author."

TOM PLAYFAIR

The story opens with 10-year-old Tom Playfair being quite a handful for his well-meaning but soft-hearted aunt. (Tom's mother has died.) Mr. Playfair decides to ship his son off to St. Maure's boarding school—an all-boys academy run by Jesuits—to shape him up, as well as to help him make a good preparation for his upcoming First Communion. Tom's adventures are just about to begin. Life at St. Maure's will not be dull!

PERCY WYNN

In this volume, Tom Playfair meets a new boy just arriving at St. Maure's. Percy Wynn has grown up in a family of 10 girls and only 1 boy—himself! His manners are formal, he talks like a book, and he has never played baseball or gone skating, boating, fishing, or even swimming! Yet he has brains, courage and high Catholic ideals. Tom and his buddies at St. Maure's befriend Percy and have a great time as they all work at turning Percy into an all-American Catholic boy.

HARRY DEE

Young Harry Dee arrives at St. Maure's thin and pale from his painful experiences involving the murder of his rich uncle. In this last book of the three, Tom and Percy help Harry recover from his early trauma—which involves solving "the mystery of Tower Hill Mansion." After many wild experiences, the three boys graduate from St. Maure's and head toward the life work to which God is calling each of them as young men.

THE TOM PLAYFAIR SERIES
By Fr. Francis J. Finn, S.J.

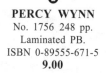

①

TOM PLAYFAIR
No. 1755 255 pp.
Laminated PB.
ISBN 0-89555-670-7
9.00

②

PERCY WYNN
No. 1756 248 pp.
Laminated PB.
ISBN 0-89555-671-5
9.00

③

HARRY DEE
No. 1757 284 pp.
Laminated PB.
ISBN 0-89555-672-3
9.00

These 3 books are the most popular of Fr. Finn's 27 Catholic novels for young people. Resembling a Catholic version of *Tom Sawyer*, these books have been read by hundreds of thousands of young people. Their quaint turn-of-the-century language is part of the charm of the stories and of Fr. Finn's own brand of humor. After young readers (or hearers) have "gotten into" his style, they find it hilarious!

But besides being fun, the stories have a moral: Tom is an unruly little boy when he is sent to St. Maure's boarding school, but after many adventures he and his friends develop into good Catholic young men and leaders—without ever losing their high spirits. (All three books feature Tom Playfair.) Young Catholics today love the Playfair books too!

1758 Set of All 3 Books. (Reg. 27.00) Only **21.00**

Prices subject to change.

At your Bookseller or direct from the Publisher.
1-800-437-5876 ***www.tanbooks.com***

Fr. Francis J. Finn, S.J. with *Dial* staff at St. Mary's College, St. Mary's, Kansas, 1894-1895.

ABOUT THE AUTHOR

Fr. Francis J. Finn, S.J.
1859-1928

THE son of Irish immigrant parents, Francis J. Finn, S.J. was born on October 4, 1859 in St. Louis, Missouri; there he grew up, attending parochial schools. As a boy, Francis was deeply impressed with Cardinal Wiseman's famous novel of the early Christian martyrs, *Fabiola*. After that, religion really began to mean something to him.

Eleven-year-old Francis was a voracious reader; he read the works of Charles Dickens, devouring *Nicholas Nickleby* and *The Pickwick Papers*. From his First Communion at age 12, Francis began to desire to become a Jesuit priest; but then his fervor cooled, his grades dropped, and his vocation might have been lost except for Fr. Charles Coppens. Fr. Coppens urged Francis to apply himself to his Latin, to improve it by using an all-Latin prayerbook, and to read good Catholic books. Fr. Finn credited the saving of his vocation to this advice and to his membership in the Sodality of Our Lady.

Francis began his Jesuit novitiate and seminary studies on March 24, 1879. As a young Jesuit scholastic, he suffered from repeated bouts of sickness. He would be sent home to recover, would return in robust health, then would come down with another ailment. Normally this would have been seen as a sign that he did not have a vocation, yet his superiors kept him on. Fr. Finn commented, "God often uses instruments most unfit to do His work."

During his seminary days Mr. Finn was assigned as prefect of St. Mary's boarding school or "college" in St. Mary's, Kansas (which became the fictional "St. Maure's"). There he learned—often the hard way—how to teach and discipline boys.

ABOUT THE AUTHOR

One afternoon while supervising a class who were busy writing a composition, Mr. Finn thought of how they represented to him the typical American Catholic boy. With nothing else to do, he took up pencil and paper. "Why not write about such boys as are before me?" he asked himself. In no time at all he had dashed off the first chapter of *Tom Playfair*. When he read it aloud to the class, they loved it! Of course they wanted more.

Francis was finally ordained to the priesthood around 1891. This was the year that *Tom Playfair* was published. Fr. Finn's publisher, Benziger Brothers, was to call *Tom Playfair* "the most successful book for boys and girls ever published in the English language." Fr. Finn would write 27 books in all, which would be translated into as many as ten languages, and even into Braille.

Fr. Finn spent many years of his priestly life at St. Xavier's in Cinncinati. There he was well loved, and it is said that wherever he went—if he took a taxi, ate at a restaurant, attended a baseball game—people would not take his money for their services, but instead would press money into his hand for his many charities. Children especially loved him. It is said that at his death in 1928, children by the thousands turned out to mourn their departed friend.

It was Fr. Finn's lifelong conviction that "One of the greatest things in the world is to get the right book into the hands of the right boy or girl. No one can indulge in reading to any extent without being largely influenced for better or worse."

According to the *American Catholic Who's Who*, Fr. Finn is "universally acknowledged the foremost Catholic writer of fiction for young people."

Photo of Fr. Finn courtesy of Midwest Jesuit Archives, St. Louis, Missouri. Biographical sketch from various sources, including an article in *Crusade* magazine which was based on Fr. Finn's memoirs as edited and published by Fr. Daniel A. Lord, S.J., in a book entitled *Fr. Finn, S.J.*